Comrade Sf
Just Mayla
in a neglected corner of a House God.
But beware! Not even arachnids, of
both spooky and sweet varieties,
are safe inside these insidious,
architectural beings. Find a tent, spin
aweb,
and foot for revolution!

ALL HAIL
THE HOUSE GODS

ANDREW J. STONE

Published by Strangehouse Books
and imprint of Rooster Republic Press LLC
www.rooosterrepublicpress.com
roosterrepublicpress@gmail.com

Copyright © Andrew J. Stone
Cover Design by Nicholas Day
Edited by Nicholas Day
Interior Design – D.F. Noble

Find our catalog at
www.roosterrepublicpress.com

PRAISE FOR *THE MORTUARY MONSTER*

"The only book in recent memory that I read, then immediately reread, then have kept peeking back at ever since, just to make sure it didn't change into something else when I wasn't looking. As deeply abnormal a narrative as you are ever likely to find, with a monster I would beat to death if I weren't so fucking sad. Awfully wonderful, and beautifully wrong. I would play baseball with *The Mortuary Monster*, and you should, too. Just watch out for the ankle violence!"
—John Skipp, author of *The Light at the End* and *The Art of Horrible People*

"Reading like a cross between *The Graveyard Book* and *High Spirits* if both had been written by Terry Southern, *The Mortuary Monster* is a madcap tumble into that tender place where death and life meet, and then try to eat one another. An odd and provocative book, and a seriously audacious debut."
—Brian Evenson, author of *A Collapse of Horses* and *Immobility*

PRAISE FOR *ALL HAIL THE HOUSE GODS*

"Fans of the bizarre and the grotesque will find plenty to enjoy in Andrew Stone's writing, but they may also find something that surprises them: a warmth, a humanity, an inventive way with language that makes the weirdness all the more persuasive. The Stone universe is too unsettling a place for most of us to feel comfortable for very long but it's a remarkably, deceptively hospitable place to visit."
—Geoff Nicholson, author of *Bleeding London and The Miranda*

"What is the use of protest? What is the purpose of fighting injustice against powers that lure you with the smell of scented candles, high ceilings, and unquestionable superiority in strength? Death is assured. And yet... as our hero in *All Hail the House Gods* awaits his ultimate sacrifice, he recounts a story of the power of the failed, doomed, and vital relationships in his rise against the Almighty structures. A joy-ride of a read, Stone has created a compelling morality tale that's moral lies somewhere in tomorrow's déjà vu. Funny, sad, stunning in its imaginative realization, Andrew J. Stone's new novel is as topical, timely, and telling as a Freudian slip."
—Laura Lee Bahr, author of *Haunt* and *Angel Meat*

"Andrew Stone writes like a laser beam shot out of a unicorn horn. His books will alter your brain in the best possible way. If an LSD Bible had babies with a hand grenade poetry collection, you'd get what Stone can do. He's dazzling."
—Brian Allen Carr, author of *Sip* and *Motherfucking Sharks*

"*All Hail the House Gods* doesn't just savagely reboot the dystopian novel with surreal flair. It strips away the most fundamentally received truths about how we live and what we live for. Truly an author to watch out for, in the most cautionary sense. Seriously, if you let him in your head, he'll wreck the place."

—Cody Goodfellow, Wonderland Award-winning author of *Sleazeland* and *All-Monster Action*

"In *All Hail the House Gods*, Andrew J. Stone has created an unsettling and terrifying alternate dimension where procreation is the ultimate patriotic duty. The writing is satirical, sinister, and unafraid to explore the uncomfortable realities of humanity. The story poses questions regarding sexual bodily autonomy and what happens when this is taken away and turned into a mechanism of self-sacrifice for your country. Stone uses gorgeous, psychedelic, and hilarious imagery to move you further and further into this world where the powerless begin to explore methods of rebellion against a power structure that kills them one by one."

—Rios de la Luz, author of Itzá

ALL HAIL
THE HOUSE GODS

ANDREW J. STONE

ACKNOWLEDGMENTS

I owe a huge amount of thanks and gratitude to Nick Day and Don Noble for taking a chance on this book. To Laura Lee Bahr and Cameron Pierce for their always welcome advice. To Rebecca Ann Jordan for inviting me to her writers' group where the idea for this story originated. To Janet Sarbanes for her initial encouragement when this book was a short story to make it longer. And last, but certainly not least, to Charlotte Simpson, Brian Allen Carr, Geoff Nicholson, Matias Viegener, Katy Quinn, Jon Wagner, Brian Evenson, and my parents for their continued support of me and my work.

All Hail the House Gods would also not exist without houses in the following cities in which I was lucky enough to write it: Hawthorne, Manhattan Beach, Gardena, El Segundo, Redondo Beach, Valencia, Seattle, Vancouver, Tijuana, Ensenada, Pretoria, Big Bend, London, Bath, and Stratford-upon-Avon.

For Lindsey, who has saved my life more times than she can ever imagine.

I

Katie wasn't always an anarchist. Or rather, as she likes to put it, a political activist. When we got married almost a decade ago, she wanted to be intimate and believed in the laws created by the Coupling Caucus just as much as any of us. And nearly a year after marriage, we gladly greeted our first child into the world.

Kurt Jr. shared my blue eyes, Katie's inwardly curved pinky fingers and, eventually, her black hair. After one of the city's Deliverers had finished coaching us through our child's birth, after she had vacated our tent, Katie held the bloody boy in her arms as silent tears streaked her cheeks.

"This is our son," she said, nuzzling her cheek against the baby's, covering her own face in blood. "Our beautiful boy."

"Yes," I agreed, my face flushed from the scene I'd just witnessed, my lips like a sagging bridge. I couldn't think of anything else to say.

Over the next month, while Katie recovered from childbirth, we spent every moment with Kurt Jr., cherishing the time we had with him before he was to be taken to the Offspring Oasis. The clearest image I have from our first son's first month of life is this: Katie held him high in her arms, making a face like a fish before popping her lips into an O, repeating this process again and again, causing our baby to fall into fits of hysterics, until, without warning, he shot a stream of urine onto my wife's face. She swore and she spat as she handed the boy to me, and he sat on my lap with the biggest toothless grin I'd ever seen. I fell in love with my son and his smile in that moment, one week after his birth, and said a silent prayer to the House Gods that he would one day have the chance to save our city.

One month later, the Collector came. His fist pressed into our tent flaps, and I let him inside. The wrinkly man approached my wife, our son's lips pressed against her node, and he said, "I have come to collect your son. His crib at the Offspring Oasis has already been prepared."

He pulled our son out of my wife's hands, separating him from his sustenance, and Kurt Jr. immediately started to sob. He stretched his arms toward his mother, and she smiled at him, whispering reassurance, but it didn't appear to appease the boy. Before the Collector stepped out of our tent, he told us the date and time of our first monthly visit to the Offspring Oasis.

Once he had left, I held Katie in my arms and we cried happy tears. We had successfully raised our son, our first one, until the time of his collection. Ever since we conceived, I was terrified that we'd do something wrong, that we wouldn't fulfill the Mandate for Mothers, and of the repercussions that could have brought to our future coupling. If we couldn't keep Kurt Jr. alive during his duration with us, how could we risk bringing more potential shame upon ourselves? How could we properly perform procreation?

The Mandate for Mothers was established shortly after our people's peace treaty with the House Gods. Before the mandate, mothers and fathers spent years looking after their children, and consequently, the time they had to themselves, to bring more potential House God fodder into the world, suffered immensely. The Mayor made it mandatory for all mothers to stop feeding their children through their nodes after the newborn's first month of life in order to keep them coupling. Ever since the mandate, no set of parents had failed to protect their offspring until the time of Collection. And now that the Collector had come, we were no exception.

The night they took Kurt Jr., Katie and I praised the House Gods with consecutive coupling. For eight years, that's how we lived. We spent our time alone together, procreating in peace, and whenever the Collector made his annual appearance, we happily handed over our offspring. And because we lived our lives for the cause, one day out of each month we were permitted to visit our children at the Offspring Oasis.

I am still standing on Harmony Crossing, shaking with anticipation and soaked in sweat. When I arrived, the sun had just begun its ascent, but now it shines directly above my head. My scalp burns red beneath the heat. I wonder if everyone who stood on this bridge had waited as long as I. Then, I wonder if anyone has. I look back at my city. My wife, Katie, waves to me. I wave to her, too. She's holding a sign and I think it says HOUSE GOD FODDER! FIGHT THE POWER AND JUMP! but I forgot my glasses at home so I'm not really sure. I wonder if pugging is frowned upon for those waiting to be sacrificed, not that it'd matter, Katie wouldn't want to even if we could.

II

Our last visit to the Offspring Oasis was nine months ago. I remember it as if it were yesterday. I awoke to the customary aroma of coffee and oysters wafting into the bedroom from the kitchen, which were separated by a curtain suspended from the ceiling. These were the sole rooms of our standard-sized tent. I sifted in and out of sleep for a few moments, wondering what kind of oysters my wife was preparing. The city's Harvesters gathered two different types of oysters from the river below the bridge, and they distributed them to the city's inhabitants. My favorite was the big, briny ones, slimy and salty as they slid down my throat. There were also tiny ones that were slightly sweet.

But then the urge to urinate dragged me out of bed. I pissed in the nearly full toilet beside our wilting headboard, praying my bladder wouldn't be full enough to cause the lumpy golden-brown liquid to rise above the brim. It wasn't, praise be to the House Gods. Once I was finished, it was full enough to flush, and I sent the day's worth of waste down into the void. Because of the severe drought we had been experiencing ever since I was born, we were only permitted to flush the toilets whenever the contents inside reached the underside of the bowl's lip. After the freshwater finished replacing the musty waste, I passed through the curtain and joined my wife at our humble table for breakfast.

After we ate our first aphrodisiacs of the day, Katie refused to pug, despite morning coupling being our mandatory duty to society. Instead, we swiftly put on our sandals and our ragged robes and rushed out of our home and into the heat of the rising sun.

Our tent had been erected a mile northwest of the bridge, and the Offspring Oasis stood one mile southwest of it. Despite the distance between us and our children, we could see their home the second we stepped through our tent flaps. The Offspring Oasis was a golden beacon on the outskirts of our flat, red wasteland of a town, a shining mountain looming over the rest of the city's gaunt residences. Holding hands, my wife and I marched toward our living children, dreaming of hearing their voices again. We only stopped when we stood parallel with the bridge, and even then, the pause was brief.

We waved to Jolene Jones, who was looking at her parents as she timidly traversed Harmony Crossing. John and Jill followed their daughter's wave, shifting their gaze from Jolene and the salivating House God before her, to us. They waved. But before they had the chance to share what a momentous occasion this was for their family, Katie and I continued our journey, and my wife told me to remind her to visit the Joneses later that night, to recruit them for what she called the Collateral Damage Collective.

Once we had passed the bridge, we made it to the Offspring Oasis without further interruption. From the outside, it appeared to stretch into eternity, and as the golden flaps swallowed us, as my wife and I anticipated seeing our children, I pretended, as I always did, that the excitement of passing through the barrier to the other side mirrored the emotions my oldest son hopefully felt as he entered the mouth of the Gothic House God nearly one year ago.

An elderly government official known as the Navigator led us down a curtained corridor, a narrow tunnel lined with vacant chairs on both sides, until we reached a fabric door, a temporary dead end. The Navigator, like all government officials working at the Offspring Oasis, was too old to reproduce. He motioned to the seats nearest the door, extending his arms into an upside down V, and Katie and I sat across from each other. Silently, the old man returned to his post at the beginning of the hallway. I started to fidget as we waited for the fabric door to open.

I chewed on the inside of my lower lip as more pairs entered the corridor. The Thompsons were the first to arrive, and the Navigator sat them beside us, and the next pair were placed beside them. I watched each new resident as they came in—neighbors, acquaintances, and even a few families from my wife's Collective—waving and smiling to them as they arrived. The anticipation of seeing my children tripled each time an additional body filled one of the corridor's empty chairs. My exhalations became increasingly rapid and my body spasmed in my seat. Across the aisle, Katie stared at me deadpan, refusing to acknowledge anyone in the hallway. Once half of the seats were occupied, an unseen hand finally unzipped the fabric door, and an old woman known as the Retriever poked her head through the opening.

"Follow me," she said, withdrawing her head. "Watch your step."

Katie and I walked through the tent flap and entered an unlit room. As the Retriever zipped the fabric door shut, the light from the hallway began to disappear, and we were enveloped in darkness. Once the door was completely zipped, lava lamps lit up the circular space, painting the canvas walls different shades of dulled purple. We walked with the Retriever halfway across the room before she motioned for us to stop. She continued her course until she reached the opposite door where she unzipped the fabric, admitting our children.

Haley, age five, entered the room first, carrying our youngest in her arms. Jude, age four, Mitch, age three, Ruthie, age two, and Paul, age one, timidly trailed her. Katie's eyes glimmered and as Paul staggered into the room she sprinted to him and swept our toddler into her arms. She nuzzled her face against his bare belly as she followed the rest of our children toward the center of the room. Haley handed Taylor to me, and our infant immediately started to sob. But before I could hand her back, Haley was already joining the group hug that had formed between my wife and the rest of our kids. I cradled the baby in my arms, swaying back and forth, attempting to cease her cries with coos. The more I rocked, the more she screamed, so I abandoned rocking her altogether and started to flick her lips instead, hoping to shock her into silence. That didn't work either, and no matter how close I got to the group hug, their voices sounded like unintelligible susurrus.

After ten minutes or so, Taylor had finally calmed down. I gently pressed her head against my heart. She was soon dozing, and I joined the family huddle, taking the place to the right of my wife.

"Jude," Katie said. "How many girls have you coupled with since the last time your father and I visited?"

Jude stuttered, clearly uncomfortable with being put on the spot before his family. "Three?" he said, barely above a whisper.

Jude always struggled with the letter "h." Consequently, it sounded like he said "tree."

"Three?" Katie asked. Her eyebrows arched slightly.

"Uh, four maybe?" Jude said, staring at his toes. "Yeah, definitely four."

"Like that's any better," Haley said, withholding a laugh.

"Jude." Katie paused, allowing silence to stress the seriousness of the situation. "You need to be coupling three or four times a day, not a month. You're not getting nearly enough practice. You have to get into the habit of constant coupling while you're still infertile, so in a few years, when you can produce soil, you won't be wasting your time learning how to pug around. You need to be inside someone the instant your body can come to completion, that way, marriage will save you from the House God lottery."

Jude nodded, still admiring his toes.

"When your father was your age, he was with at least three different girls a day."

"Actually," I said, covering Taylor's ear opposite my chest with my free hand, trying to keep my voice from waking her, "I only coupled about once a week until—"

"Never mind your father's shortcomings," Katie said. "Next time we see you, I want you to have coupled at least once a day, understand?"

"Yes, mom," Jude said.

"Look at me," Katie said, her eyes glazed. "I love you, son. And although I hate to admit it, the only way you'll be safe is through procreation. And I can't lose..."

Katie cut herself off and addressed Haley. Taylor woke up and resumed crying, and my family exiled me from the huddle. As I hushed our youngest child, I wished Katie would couple with me as often as she encouraged our children to with strangers. I wished she would couple with me at all. But no matter how many times I complimented her, no matter how many times I reminded her of our past pleasures, she wouldn't let me inside her. I tried to remember the last time we climaxed together, but the occasion eluded me. As I pondered our nonexistent foundation, the fabric door our children came through was unzipped, and the Retriever returned to collect our kids.

Haley took Taylor away from me, and in her older sister's arms, the infant stopped wailing. How had thirty minutes already passed? This couldn't have been more than thirty seconds. Regardless, our children were nearly through the tent flaps, and Katie was encouraging Haley to remind her siblings to pug as often as she was, which meant at least twice a day. I proclaimed my love to my children, but before they could return the declaration, the fabric door had zipped them away.

III

My wife always said that the only reason she loved visiting the Offspring Oasis was to hear our children's voices, but I like to think that there was another reason for her happiness, too. Because if it weren't for the Offspring Oasis, particularly the Green Room within, we would have never wed. At the time of our marriage, which, without exception, coincides with proof of conception, I was twelve years old. Katie was thirteen.

When I arose from bed that morning one hundred and eleven months ago, I had no intentions of being engaged mere hours into my day. Groggily, I stumbled out the sleeping quarters, which was located in the center of the Offspring Oasis, alongside twenty-four other boys with whom I shared the bedroom. We staggered deeper into the tent toward the cafeteria for our morning aphrodisiacs. We were served avocado slices mashed on bread, figs, and honeyed bananas. We drank either coffee or chai tea. Once we had eaten just enough to energize us, and not a bite more, so as to avoid the risk of entering a food coma, we exited the cafeteria, each of us choosing between a variety of doors, each option leading to a separately themed room where we were to spend the next several hours participating in what the government officials called Erotic Recreation.

Most boys with whom I shared sleeping arrangements walked into the Red Room that day, but for reasons I could not, and still cannot comprehend, I decided, at the last minute, to leave my roommates and play in the Green Room. The moment I stepped inside, I knew I had made the right choice. I had only played inside the Green Room a few times before because all my friends preferred the others, and as a result, I always forgot how wonderful this place was. Unlike the Red Room, which was heated by pits of fire spread across the red dirt floor, mirroring the landscape our parents described as their home whenever they visited, the Green Room was covered in trimmed grass, strawberry plants, and fig trees. Unlike the Purple Room, which was heavily scented in lavender, lighted by lava lamps, and covered in different shades of purple carpet from its floor to its ceiling, the Green Room was full of fresh air and, because it has an open roof, lighted by the sun. Unlike the Blue Room, which consisted entirely of water, this room had a murky-green, oval-shaped pond in its center, making it the only other recreational room with water.

Overwhelmed by the beauty of the Green Room, some time passed before I noticed the other bodies inside it, but when I did, I saw her immediately: The girl with the halo above her head. She swayed beneath a fig tree, pressing its fruit into her mouth with one hand, while the other was pulling her dark mahogany curly-carpet hair, expanding and contracting her furry furnace. Her face was the color of the moon, her eyes hazel, and the hair on her head long and black. Her nodes were petite, tiny craters shimmering in the sun. My plank grew rock hard. I stepped over the pair coupling on the floor before her, my body boiling as I approached.

After what felt like decades, I finally reached the glimmering girl. As I got closer, she somehow seemed to multiple herself because there were now three of her vibrating from side to side. I moved my lips toward the center of her three pairs, but she pressed a finger against mine, pausing my advance. I asked her what was wrong, and she kneeled before me. She closed her lips around my chain and everything around us seemed to intensify. As she used her tongue to sweep up any potential soil, the scents of the falling figs clogged my nostrils, and the songs of the birds buzzed in my ears. The buds of her tongue sent vibrations through my body, and moments later, she slid my entire plank into her mouth, pressing her nose against my carpet.

I had coupled with dozens of girls before this one, but none of them had ever done anything like this. Previously, coupling had always been an act of civil obedience, something we did not for pleasure, but for safety and security. But as this girl's lips danced up and down my plank, she taught me something new about coupling—that it could create love.

Just as the epiphany of love struck, she removed her mouth from my tower and lay on her back. I fell on top of her and pushed my plank between her furry furnace. I slid all the way inside of her free of friction. I'd never before been inside of a girl this wet near the end of intercourse, never mind the beginning. Consequently, for this reason, or maybe because of the magic she had done with her mouth, I soiled six seconds later.

"Why'd you stop?" she asked.

I was still inside her, but I had ceased thrusting. "I umm...," I said.

"Already?"

I nodded. My cheeks burned, and my forehead started to sweat. I had never felt embarrassed about pugging before.

"Should we check?" she asked.

"Right," I said. "I mean, yes." I can't believe I had forgotten about the post-couple check. When I had pugged in the past, the check was my favorite part of the act, but with this girl the protocol hadn't even occurred.

We held hands as she stood and spread her legs. We watched her furry furnace intently, waiting, as government officials had repeatedly instructed, to see if anything white leaked out. The anticipation was killing me. I had never produced soil before, and I feared that if I had failed to do so once again, I would lose my shot at spending my life with the most amazing girl I had ever met.

Minutes passed. Sweat slid down my face as if I were in a sauna. I prepared to admit my reproductive shortcomings. But the second I spoke, she shushed me. That's when she pointed at her furnace.

"Do you see it?" she asked.

"No," I said, shaking my head.

"It's right there!" she hollered. "Soil!"

"It is?" I couldn't believe it. Had I finally done it?

"Are you making fun of me?" she asked.

"No," I almost shouted. I was horrified that she thought I might be making fun of her at a time like this. If what she said was true, this was the happiest moment of my life. Not only did I actually, finally produce soil, but I did it with the girl I had fallen hopelessly in love with, despite having just met her and despite not even knowing her name. "I really don't see it," I said. Then I added, "But I believe you."

"Are you blind?" she asked. She sounded sincere.

And that's when I realized I was in dire need of glasses. "I'm not blind," I said, defensively, "but I think I might need glasses."

She used her finger to scoop up the soil supposedly drooling out of her furnace, and lifted the substance right in front of my eyes. "See it now?" she asked.

"Yes," I said, and I did see it, and it was wondrous. "Should we go show the Green Room Guardians?"

"Not yet," she said. "I'm Katie Mara." She extended a slimy hand to shake.

"Kurt Nolan," I said, "and handshakes are for strangers." I ignored her outstretched hand and hugged her. I figured that since we would be engaged when we showed the Guardians where my secondhand soil came from, she wouldn't mind the gesture.

Katie embraced me as warmly as I embraced her, and together we fell to the grass and cuddled for a few moments. It felt like mere seconds had passed when Katie ended our embrace, saying, "Let's go show the Guardians."

"Okay," I agreed, slowly rising to my feet.

"Want to hold hands?" she asked.

"I could see well enough to make it this far," I said, neck, cheeks, and forehead burning red, "I think I can make it just a little bit further."

"I meant because I want to hold your hand," she said. "I know you don't need to, but I want to."

I could have died. My entire body must have been lobster red because I burned everywhere, as if I had just eaten a militia of chili peppers. I tried to say that would be lovely, but all I could do was nod. I extended my hand and our fingers enlaced, and Katie led me toward the Guardians of the Green Room.

After the Guardians confirmed that there was indeed soil slowly dripping out of Katie, they declared us engaged and, sans enthusiasm, shot confetti into the air via party poppers while congratulating us. They handed me a slip of purple paper. Across the top, in bold black letters, it declared "Certificate of Engagement." Automatically, I passed the paper to Katie. The Guardians instructed us to hand the paper to the officials on the other side of the Green Room's door, which we did. After the second set of officials had scanned the paper, they returned it with stoic congratulations, and one of them proceeded to lead us toward our Engagement Room, which they said was located in the Village of the Engaged. I had never heard of this Village of the Engaged, and when I asked Katie about it, she said she never had, either.

"The Village of the Engaged," the official said, apparently not caring that no one had asked him, "is where we house pairs who are awaiting proof of conception. For your convenience, it is located within the confines of the Offspring Oasis, just a little further from the main cafeteria than the dorms where you were previously residing. Again, for your convenience, the Village of the Engaged has its own cafeteria. This maximizes the time you two will spend in your room together as you practice procreating in peace while you await your results."

"But if we're constantly coupling in the Village of the Engaged," I said, "won't that increase our chances of conceiving? And if we conceive, won't it be impossible to know whether we did so in the Green Room or in the Engagement Room?"

"Bababababa," he said, lifting a finger to his lips. "No asking questions."

I rolled my eyes. Katie looked at me.

"Wait," she said, stopping, which caused the rest of us to stop.

"In the name of the House Gods, why are you stopping?"

"Because," Katie said, fearless, "my fiancé needs glasses."

She was pointing to the optometrist's office, which we had just happened to pass. Her bravery surprised and impressed me.

"Is this true?" the official asked me.

"Uh, yeah," I said.

"How many fingers am I holding up?"

"Three," I said, confident in my answer.

"Fucking imbecile," the official muttered, shaking his head. "The answer is one."

I shrugged.

"See?" Katie asked.

"Very well," the official said, and he led us to the optometrist.

IV

A strong breeze blows by and Harmony Crossing sways. It's a skinny wooden bridge, much too small for a house to stand on. But every morning, as the sun rises, one sacrifice is to wait in the center of Harmony Crossing for a group of House Gods to gather before the trees on the other side. Once the House Gods have gathered, they summon the sacrifice, who then walks into death to keep our city safe. If the day ever comes when the House Gods gather at Harmony Crossing before their fodder is ready for slaughter, they will declare war on my people again. As I stand on the swaying bridge, the first House God crabwalks out from the trees and into the open space of grass before me. It's a single-story brick house with a blood red door, and I prepare for the honor of being sacrificed by waving to the House God as a smile slowly spreads across my face.

The last time I saw a sacrifice, thirteen months before our final visit to the Offspring

Oasis, I held Katie with my left arm and a sign above our heads with my right. The sign said KURT JR. YOU MAKE US SO PROUD. Between my son's bravery on Harmony Crossing and the baby bump my wife sported, my smile couldn't be any wider. As we waited for more House Gods to arrive—there were currently only four in the clearing beneath the stretch of trees on the other side of the bridge—the muscles in and around my mouth started to hurt. The pain grew as the moment stretched, and as more House Gods trickled into view, I still couldn't stop smiling.

"Do you think little Kurt knows how happy he is making us?" I asked Katie.

"I don't know," she said, looking up at me, revealing a small smile of her own. "I think he probably thinks he is just doing his duty. That's probably it. I mean, what else could he be thinking?"

"Little Kurt," I cried, and as our son looked over his shoulder, I pointed at our sign. I added, "We love you."

He nodded. He opened his mouth to say something to us, but the wind against our backs blew his words away from us back toward him and the House Gods.

The pain in my face grew as more House Gods arrived. Eventually, the last House God appeared on the other side of Harmony Crossing, and as they summoned our son in unison, saying, "All hail the House Gods," and as Kurt Jr. began to walk toward them, something inside my wife went completely haywire.

"Kurt Jr.," she cried, "come to mama!"

She slithered away from me, and I immediately dropped the sign. Just before she stepped onto Harmony Crossing, I wrapped my arms around her and dragged her back a few feet. She swatted at and pushed against my face. She smudged my glasses, and they kept her fingers from poking my eyes. But no matter how hard she hit me, I refused to release her.

Kurt Jr. walked hesitatingly at first, but after a few steps, all the training from the Offspring Oasis and the House God's homey scents kicked in, and his slow walk quickly turned to swift skips. In addition to coupling, while living in the Offspring Oasis, children spend a few hours each day skipping across model bridges toward the scents of peppermint and gingerbread, of campfires and cedar, training them for the act of sacrifice in case they are ever lucky enough to win the lottery. Consequently, our son skipped toward the open door of a House God likely without the slightest thought as to where his body was leading him.

"Kurt," Katie said, growing increasingly hysteric, "our son is going to die, and it's all my fault."

I nodded, and she smacked my nose. Blood rolled out of my nostrils and dripped into my mouth. It took all my strength to continue keeping her from rushing the bridge to interfere with our son's sacrifice, a crime punishable by death via sacrifice. Katie hit my nose again. I heard a crunch. My mind started to spin, and my nose felt like it was simultaneously freezing and on fire. I wished I could let go of her to check if it were still straight. I wiped the blood covering my chin on the back of her robe, and I thought my wife had seriously misunderstood the meaning of the government's letter.

A few months prior to this honorable occasion, while Katie and I were guzzling our nighttime aphrodisiacs—chai tea with whipped cream, a watermelon arugula salad topped with pine nuts and pumpkin seeds, and a few chocolate covered strawberries—I jumped at the sight of fist flesh pressing against the canvas door of our tent, and I bumped the kitchen table and knocked over our chai teas in the process. My wife scowled at me. I shrugged. She pointed to the pile of towels pressed against the curtain separating our kitchen from our bedroom as she made her way toward the flaps of the tent. The fist from the other side continued to send ripples throughout our home.

"Coming," Katie called. She sounded annoyed.

By the time she unzipped the flaps, I had returned to the table with a dirty towel in hand. As I mopped up the mess, I peered through the crack in the canvas my wife had created. On the other side of the door stood the most massive man I've ever seen. Both Katie and I could walk through our open tent flaps standing perfectly straight. But even if this stranger shaped his body like a rainbow, his hunched back would still scrape the ceiling. But Katie didn't invite him in, and he never tried to take a step toward us. Instead, he simply slipped an envelope into my wife's hands and left without saying a word.

The letter was addressed to the parents of Kurt Nolan Jr. In its entirety, it read:

Early this morning, the card containing the name Kurt Nolan Jr. was randomly selected from the Deck of Eligible Children. We can only imagine the joy this announcement must bring you, and because of your consistent service to our city through the creation of not only this boy, but your other fine offspring whose names remain in the Deck of Eligible Children, we cordially invite you to attend the sacrifice of your son, which will take place eighty-nine days from today.

With gratitude,
The Coupling Caucus

Katie and I were elated. Ever since we first held Kurt Jr. in our arms, we had been anxiously awaiting this moment, fearing it would never come. But because of our diligent coupling, we now had the honor of protecting our people from the vicious House Gods by creating a child who would soon be sacrificed.

Katie threw the letter to the ground and pushed me toward our room. Backpedaling, I moved through the hanging curtain and lost my balance as I tripped over the foot of our bed. Katie jumped on top of me. She was already so wet that I easily slid inside. A few minutes later we were both lying on our backs with big grins. We leaned into each other and shared a sweaty kiss. We didn't know it yet, but the night we learned of our son's looming sacrifice was the same night we conceived the last child we would ever have.

Katie didn't stop struggling to free herself from my embrace until after Kurt Jr. had disappeared inside of the mouth of the Gothic House God. I let go of her as the House God closed its front door, swallowing our son. She collapsed to her knees and wept. As the dust rose from the impact of her fall, I tried to comfort my wife by laying my hands on her shoulders. She lashed her arms at me and I leapt back, hoping to protect my nose from another punch. She told me to leave her the fuck alone, and then she stared at the Gothic House God that had eaten our son.

I stepped beside Katie and studied her face as she gazed across Harmony Crossing. After a few minutes, a change overcame her eyes. It's nothing I can explain in words, but one moment they appeared dead, dazed, and the next, they looked terrified, like the eyes of a child who has just woken from a nightmare and is still unconvinced that she had been dreaming. But that's still not quite right. At any rate, I followed her eyes and found Kurt Jr. on the other side of the Gothic House God's window. Our son was scraping away the maroon curtains and screaming, begging us for a second chance at life, but what could we do?

V

A second House God comes into my view. It consists entirely of glass and I can see straight through it to the trees beyond. Inside its mouth everything looks metallic. Despite the intense heat of the sun, a shiver crawls up my spine, causing the tiny hairs covering my body to stand tall for a few seconds. I don't remember how many House Gods there were when my wife and I saw the sacrifice of our son, but the two houses before me fill the field of grass like two specs of sand in the sea. And the sun now shines so strongly, I can feel my skin becoming raw. I don't know how much longer I can wait here for the House Gods to summon me. The water below Harmony Crossing is starting to seep into my mind like a sickness, the sound of the rapids rolling over the rocks, calling me away from my role as sacrifice.

On the way home from our son's sacrifice, Katie told me she wanted to get rid of the child growing inside of her.

"How?" I asked. I had never heard of such a thing.

"I don't know," she admitted, and silent tears swam down red cheeks.

I nodded. We continued our mile trek toward our tent, each step falling slower than the last. Our legs felt like coagulated honey crawling through the desert sand. My wife's tears kept rolling out of her eyes. Katie was the strongest person I knew, and I didn't know what to say to cheer her up. I figured she'd stop sobbing soon. Surely her tear ducts must be nearly empty now. But the longer we walked, the faster her tears fell.

By the time we had trudged halfway to our tent, Katie vowed, "We will never make another child for as long as we live."

"But the Coupling Caucus," I said, "what will we do when they come to make their annual progress report?"

"We will figure that out when the time comes, Kurt. But first, we need to get rid of this child inside me. We need to protect this baby from stumbling into the same fate as our beautiful boy."

"But Kurt Jr. did his duty," I said. I had no idea what Katie was actually saying, but it certainly wasn't what I was hearing. I made a mental note to get my ears checked by the doctor later in the week. "He bravely sacrificed himself for the rest of humankind.

We should be proud of our coming child's potential, not protective."

"You really are a fucking idiot," she said, and her tears stormed from her face to the floor. "Do you not see how pointless all of this is? Do you not see that we are breeding children with the sole purpose of preparing mindless sacrifices for the greedy House Gods? Do you not see that our offspring are dying, and the only way we can save them is to dispose of them, is to keep them from coming out of me?"

I didn't know what to say. My ears had to be broken. Surely my wife couldn't be this callous toward the Coupling Caucus. Without them, our species would have been wiped out centuries ago during the House God War. But as we walked further and further away from Harmony Crossing, I began to doubt the shortcoming of my ears. After all, I could hear my wife's cries loud and clear. Besides, she wouldn't be sobbing this much over a joyous occasion. If she were this miserable, she had to have said something along the lines of what I had heard. As this began to settle in my mind, I tried to understand my wife's reactions to our son's sacrifice, but no matter how hard I thought, her tears and her words remained nonsensical.

We passed one tattered canvas teepee tent after another as we made our way home. The tents belonging to the older couples tended to have weathered holes from sandstorms, sometimes patched but typically unattended. When we reached our own shabby beige tent, the sky turned pink as the setting sun sank closer to the horizon. I unzipped the flaps and let my wife inside. She stormed through the kitchen, whisking away the curtain, and collapsed in our bed. She was lying flat on her stomach before the curtain had straightened itself. Once my wife was concealed in our bedroom, I began to make us dinner.

I heated up some oyster soup and once it started to simmer, I added lemon juice and chili peppers. I poured two bowls and carefully carried our dinner past the curtain and into our bedroom. I sat on the edge of the bed and passed my wife's bowl to her. We ate our soups in silence, and when we were finished, I carried our bowls to the kitchen and left them in the sink. I walked back to the bedroom with my plank rising. Our dinner aphrodisiacs were already working their way through my body. But when I got into bed, my wife was already asleep. Or she was pretending to be asleep. I wasn't really sure.

Either way, we did not pug that night. It was the first night since our engagement that we failed to procreate after our final serving of aphrodisiacs, and I didn't know what to do. What if the city found out? Would they sacrifice us for failing to follow the law? Or did we have to miss more than a single coupling to be sent to Harmony Crossing?

To distract myself from my thoughts, I left our tent and went to the place where they hosted the city-sponsored card games. The Flaps of Fate was built a mile north from our tent, in the opposite direction of the

Offspring Oasis, and when I stepped inside the golden, glimmering tent, I already felt a little bit better. Because it was so late, only a few tables were occupied. I joined the table with the most players, assuming they had most recently begun their game. I won the first hand, and I almost forgot that I should have been in bed with my wife in post-couple slumber.

I spent two hours every day at the city-sponsored card games gambling for the fate of my kids ever since Katie and I were married and had moved into our own tent. Katie used to play with me, but the night before our oldest son was selected for sacrifice, my wife was the first player at our table eliminated from the game, and she had sworn off cards ever since.

Unfortunately, I failed to win the table that night, which would have cancelled out my wife's loss. Instead, John Jones won. As a result, all the cards that would have been bearing the names of John's children in the next day's lottery were replaced with our kids' names. Luckily, John was a few years younger than us, and thus, he just had two children. This meant that only the names of our oldest two kids, Kurt Jr. and Haley, would appear twice in the Deck of Eligible Children. If John and his wife had begotten more babies than us, then all our offspring would have been put in the deck at least twice, and the older ones would have had three cards to their name, not that it made any difference.

Twice was all Kurt Jr. needed to win the lottery.

VI

One week after the death of our first son, the meetings started.

I had just returned from a series of unfortunate hands at the city-sponsored card games, and when I entered our tent, fearing my wife's reaction to my losses, I was greeted by an aphrodisiac feast like I'd never seen before. I completely forgot about cards as the scent of oyster soup simmered next to half a dozen or so boiling artichokes. There were a few large bowls full of watermelon arugula salad, and beside the greens, there was a bread spread: Bread soaked in olive oil, bread smeared with mashed avocado, and bread piled beneath bananas slathered in honey. For dessert, my wife had prepared a platter of chocolate covered strawberries and a cherry, pomegranate, and whipped cream blend. In addition to the food, she had made a few pots of coffee and a few jugs of chai tea lattes. I licked my lips. I hoped this meant Katie had finally come to her senses and planned to couple with me later this evening.

"What's the special occasion?" I asked, hoping she'd confirm my suspicions.

"You'll see," she said, refusing to turn around. She was too busy studying the simmering soup to greet me.

I stood behind my wife, breathing down onto the top of her head. My cheeks puffed out, eyebrows squeezed together. After a minute, she still hadn't turned around, so I quietly grunted. She turned off the stove and faced me.

"For fuck's sake," she said, and she looked annoyed, "stop pouting and just sit at the table already. You'll see what all this fuss is about soon enough."

I poured two cups of coffee before sitting in my seat. A minute later, my wife brought over two bowls of oyster soup. She returned to the stove, retrieved an artichoke along with a cup of melted butter, and set the plant between our plates. I peeled a petal and dipped it in butter before scraping off the meat with my teeth. It was the best artichoke I had ever had. I told my wife as much.

She exhaled relief. "I was nervous," she admitted, "I never boiled them before. I was afraid I'd mess it all up and they'd think I was a lousy cook."

Before I had the chance to ask my wife what she meant by "they," a knock came to our door. I sat stiff, frozen by the sight of meat meeting canvas as if I'd never seen open palms press into tent flaps before, but my wife immediately got up from the table as if this sort of thing happened every evening.

She greeted the group at the door, about twenty people or so, and invited them inside. Some of the strangers apologized for intruding when they realized we were in the middle of dinner, and just as I was going to tell them off, saying something about the laws forbidding pairs from socializing with other pairs outside of the Offspring Oasis and city-sponsored card games, Katie told them they weren't intruding at all. Then she even said that we were expecting them, that she'd made dinner for all of them, too. I was so shocked that all I could think was that we didn't have room to seat any of them. After all, our table was built for no more than two at a time. But once our guests received their food, they just sat on the floor, waiting. I had no idea what they were expecting, but Katie quickly relieved my confusion and their curiosity.

My wife proclaimed, "Thank you all for coming. My husband and I are so glad you could make it on such short notice." Katie said this as if I were in on some secret, as if she had shared her schemes with me. "We created the Collateral Damage Collective as a platform for weekly meetings to brainstorm ways to resist the House Gods and the policies of our people. Ever since the houses on the other side of Harmony Crossing became alive and ate those living inside of their walls over five hundred years ago, ever since the House Gods waged war on our people and the Mayor at the time created the Coupling Caucus, which presented the sacrifice system as a peace treaty, our people, our children, have been enslaved by the House Gods. We are sick of bringing children into this world for the sole purpose of sacrifice. We are tired of being unable to bring our children home."

The group erupted in applause. In order to fit in, I clapped with them, although I wasn't entirely sure I was pleased with how the night was developing.

My wife continued, "Tonight we will each introduce ourselves and share what brought us here. Tonight is all about getting to know each other. Next week, the resistance will start. My husband and I will show you what I mean."

My wife motioned for me to stand beside her, and I obliged. She told these strangers who I was and how many children we had made as well as their names and ages. She never gave me a chance to speak, which was a blessing, because I had nothing to say to these people. Once she had finished our story, the visitors applauded again, and we resumed sitting across from each other at our table.

A man and a woman nearest the front tent flaps rose next. The man said, "My name is Tucker Thompson and this here is my wife Millie," he motioned to his wife, who stood beside him.

Millie said, in a voice barely above a whisper, "It's so nice to be here."

Tucker continued, "We have six children: Raven, Samantha, Tommy, Bret, Bert, and Skyler. Bret and Bert are twins, and our youngest and oldest were eaten by the House Gods exactly one week apart late last year. Since then, we promised each other that no more of our kin would die inside the walls of those inhuman bastards."

As we sat there, crammed in our kitchen, we applauded Tucker and Millie, who was just starting to show signs of her seventh pregnancy. I took this time to sneak toward the sink and pour myself a chai tea latte from the jug on the counter. Before I could cap off my cup, my wife asked me to refill our guests' mugs. As the next pair started to speak, I walked the jug around the room.

"I'm Janet," Janet said.

"And I'm Jordan," said Jordan.

"We're the Steeles," Janet continued, "and we have two daughters: Jane and Elise. Jane is two and Elise is just two months. We used to have a son..."

Janet started crying uncontrollably and her husband's voice chimed in. "We used to have a son," he said, "but two days ago he sacrificed himself to the House Gods. He was only a year old." Tears ran down his cheeks. "And we did nothing to save him."

I couldn't clap with the rest of the Collective because I was still refilling their drinks. But I was thankful for this inability because it felt like an entirely inappropriate time for applause. Nine more pairs introduced themselves over the next ninety minutes, but I spaced out and immediately forgot their names as well as anything else they had to say.

Seven lattes later, my wife's voice filled the room again. She was saying, "It was great getting to know each of you and hearing a little of your stories. It's because of these stories, and the millions like them of those who continue to couple blindly, that we have created the CDC. Consequently, if any member who is not currently carrying a potential sacrifice becomes pregnant, she and her husband will face expulsion. From this day onward, not one of us or our children will die at the doors of the House Gods without them having to face severe collateral damage. Goodnight."

The moment the last lingering pair left our tent, Katie reached across the table, pulled me to my feet, and kissed me hard. As she slid her tongue between my lips, she used her arm to sweep all the empty plates to the floor before climbing onto the table. She wrapped her legs around my thighs and told me to couple her.

Fucking finally, I thought, my wife wants me again, wants to keep us safe again. I lifted my robe over my head as my wife scrunched up hers around her waist. She grabbed my plank and pulled me inside of her furry furnace. But before I could get into a consistent groove, she grabbed my shoulders and ceased my thrusts.

"Promise me you'll pull out?"

I nodded. Although we would still be breaking the law by preventing ourselves from procreating, the intimacy of coupling made me feel a lot safer. This way, we at least had the pretense of procreation to make me feel like we were following the law. Though I didn't truly understand why it mattered whether or not I pulled out. I mean, she was already three months pregnant.

"Even though I'm already pregnant," she said, as if she had read my mind, "we cannot get in the habit of coupling to completion, okay?"

I nodded again, amazed at my wife's apparent abilities, and she moved her hands from my shoulders down to my gully. Six seconds later, I climaxed, shooting my soil onto her stomach.

Maybe it's because, for the first time in as long as I can remember, I went a whole week without coupling. Maybe it's because the way my wife came onto me so forcefully the second we were alone. Whatever the reason, the power of this orgasm pressed my thoughts into the past, back to the first time I had ever made love outside of the Erotic Recreation rooms in the Offspring Oasis.

Katie and I had just settled into our tiny tent in the Village of the Engaged. Aside from the full-sized bed, which rested against the back wall, there was a sink to the left of the bed and a toilet to its right. Katie leapt into the bed and, lying on her back, spent a few seconds making a blanket angel. I stood just inside the zipped flaps, fidgeting. For the first time in my life, I was in a tent with a girl unobserved by my peers and the city's employees. It certainly didn't help that Katie had started sliding her middle finger in and out of her furnace, creating a louder suctioning sound with each insertion. Despite the discomfort, and despite the fact that Katie and I had just coupled in the Green Room, my plank started to grow harder than it ever had before. Katie slid a second finger inside of herself, and with her free hand, she beckoned me toward her.

My heart hammered against my chest and my hands and feet became clammy, but my legs slowly carried me forward. I kneeled on the edge of the bed before trying to lie beside my fiancée, but whenever I lowered myself toward the comforter, she rolled beneath me. After a few failed attempts, I abandoned my discomfort as best I could, and our bodies pressed together like the bricks of a house.

As our lips met and we shared saliva, I had never felt more naked in my life. Of course, I had never worn clothes before. Clothing is banned until marriage, and after the ceremony, each spouse is provided with a few robes. But it wasn't the lack of clothes that made me feel naked, it was the lack of eyes. Without being watched, everything was more real, more intimate. When our tongues met, I could feel the bumps of her taste buds as they rubbed against mine, spreading the flavor of her oyster breakfast mixed with my pre-soil from our time in the Green Room a few hours earlier. As I rubbed my plank against her cleat, her protruding flesh stroked my shaft. Every nerve ending prickled with pleasure. The faster I slid up and down her cleat, the louder she moaned. She told me to press into her harder, and I did. Her back arched, curving her upper body into a rainbow. She tilted back her head and moaned again.

Lying flat once more, my fiancée grabbed my plank and guided me inside of her furnace. The thought of doing our societal duty, of keeping our city safe by creating a potential sacrifice, never even crossed my mind. Instead, all the training I went through in the Offspring Oasis, all the ideas I was taught about coupling, were flushed down my mental toilet. My mind was blank. Most my body was devoid of feeling. My entire existence was contained in the sensations passing through my plank, until they passed through me and into my fiancée. We moaned together, and I collapsed on top of her.

Exhausted, shiny with sweat, we slipped into sleep.

VII

Eight days after my wife created the Collateral Damage Collective, I had the best hour of cards of my life. I was on fire. I won nearly every hand. But after an hour of winning, my chips began to drift to the piles of those around me. This wasn't because my luck with the dealer had finally faltered, but rather, it was because of the strange ideas that were being spread by one of the players with whom I shared the table.

The first hand I lost, I was dealt two aces. After the flop, there were two two's on the table, one of which was a club, as well as a six of clubs. The turn produced a four of clubs, and I didn't even notice what came with the river, but it wasn't a two. Instead of folding after failing to secure a full house, instead of realizing that someone must have had a straight flush, I kept on mindlessly matching the other players' raises. Despite losing half my winnings in a single hand, I wore a smile wider than the woman who had just taken my chips.

Devin Anderson, who still had far fewer chips than me, was saying, "There are many House Gods against the lottery system. These House Gods never eat humans, and they think their fellow Houses are horrible for allowing us through their front doors." He was dead serious. He swore by what he said.

At first, I thought Devin was just trying to distract anyone who would listen so he wouldn't be the first one at the table to lose all his chips. But even after he lost, even after his children's odds at winning the lottery the next day had been increased, he still insisted that some House Gods were fighting for human rights, for human liberation. As my chips continued to dwindle, Devin even argued that just because plenty of House Gods didn't protest on our behalf, that didn't mean they preferred eating us over furniture. He claimed that most House Gods were good.

When I walked through the front flaps of our tent, excited to share all that I had heard about the House Gods with my wife, I found her silently crying on the kitchen floor. Her teeth were clamped onto an oyster shell, an unscrewed and straightened metal robe hanger was trembling in her hand, and a puddle of blood was pouring out from between her legs. I grabbed every towel in our tent and wrapped them around my wife like a diaper, trying to stop the bleeding, trying to erase her pain.

The night before, during the CDC's second meeting, Millie Thompson told us a tale about her mother's mother's best friend, Tess, who was sacrificed to the House Gods for trying to keep her baby from coming out of her furnace. Millie said that Tess unscrewed one of her metal robe hangers and straightened it like a spear. She fished around her furnace with the hanger, stabbing the baby again and again. A few minutes after the sword fight had begun, the river of blood seeping out of Tess carried tiny clumps of baby with it. She fainted. When her husband found her later that night, unconscious and covered in blood, he immediately left to fetch a doctor. The doctor said Tess had bled out during the procedure, that there was nothing she could do to revive her.

Millie explained that in order to keep other pairs from copying this procedure, from trying to terminate their offering to society, the city decided to make an example of the deceased Tess and her heartbroken husband.

One week after Tess's death, the House Gods received their first and, as far as I'm aware, only double sacrifice to date. Tess's husband carried his dead wife over his shoulders as he walked across Harmony Crossing toward the mouth of a hungry House God. Attendance for the other pairs was mandatory. Everyone needed to witness what would happen if a family tried to rob the House Gods from a potential meal. They did. Seeing the pair trudge across the bridge, seeing Tess's mutilated furnace, kept those in attendance from reenacting the operation. And aside from the memories of those who were old enough to attend the sacrifice, Tess's procedure was erased from history. Sure, a few families whose bloodline directly connected them to the event still secretly passed the story down from one generation to the next, but no one had ever tried to terminate future House God fodder again. This changed when I entered our tent and saw my wife looking oyster pale.

To be clear, Millie was not suggesting any of the pregnant mothers in the CDC attempt this procedure. Rather, she was offering up the idea that if any of the members' children are chosen as fodder, one of the child's parents should volunteer to reenact the day of the double sacrifice by carrying their kid through the door of a House God. This parent would have a homemade bomb strapped to their body beneath their robe. Our ancestors used various bombs against the House Gods during the war, and any of them would work. As this parent and their child entered the front door, they would detonate the bomb, taking the House God down with them.

Generally, this idea was received very well by the constituents of the Collective. Some even said they would start researching bombs that night. But as I heard Millie's story, I thought about my wife's previous promise of getting rid of our coming child. I meant to talk about it with her when we were alone, but as she had done after the first meeting of the CDC, the second the last pair left our tent, she pounced on me. If she could love me with such passion immediately after hearing Millie's story, then I somehow convinced myself that she had abandoned all thoughts of terminating her pregnancy. But I should have known. I should have resisted her seduction and spoken to her about Millie's story.

My tears mirrored Katie's as I worked to keep the blood from coming, as I cleaned up my wife. After the bleeding had stopped, after I brought her a cup of water, she cried, "I cannot let this baby out of me, Kurt. I have to protect our coming child from the lottery."

"I know," I said, even though I didn't know how preventing the baby's birth amounted to protection. I wished I knew how to convey to my wife what I had heard, that not all House Gods were bad, that some might even be good. I wished I could say we can keep the baby because one day, our child would live in a world free from the lottery system. But it was too late, and even if it weren't, I doubted she would've believed me. Instead, I simply said, "What's done is done."

She nodded. We hugged. Except this wasn't over. As the months passed, Katie's belly grew more and more bulbous.

Katie gave birth to Taylor six months later.

VIII

Three months after my wife founded the CDC, on the night of the thirteenth meeting, Janet and Jordan Steele arrived in a state of total delirium. Janet was sporting a brand-new baby bump. She looked stunning as she shivered, and I immediately started to sweat.

Janet swore on the lives of all her children that, in agreement with what the members of the CDC had previously decreed, her husband didn't shoot his soil inside of her. Jordan added that this was some kind of miraculous mistake. Everyone believed Janet and Jordan. Everyone felt sympathetic for their familial addition. Even so, Katie promptly expelled them from the group, announcing that Janet and Jordan Steele had officially become baby killers.

Janet cried. Jordan threatened that he'd inform the city about the CDC's mission and its meetings.

My wife said, "If you become an informant for the city, not only will you prove us right in removing you from the Collective, you will also prove that you never cared about your children's lives, that you never cared for human life altogether." She wasn't angry. She wasn't panicked. She sounded matter-of-fact. She continued, "Unlike the members of the Coupling Caucus and other city officials, and unlike those who still procreate in peace, you have undergone an awakening; you understand the value of human life and human decency. To revert to the old ways after your enlightenment would make you worse than the very worst House God to have ever existed."

Jordan stared at my wife wordlessly as he transformed himself into a bobble head. After all the anti-House God propaganda he had been spewing the last three months, what else could he have done? Before he and his wife left our tent, he tried to regain some dignity. He said that he and his wife would still work to overthrow the House Gods as silent allies of the Collateral Damage Collective. Katie nodded her consent. Jordan and Janet crept out of our tent. The thirteenth meeting was finally going to begin.

During the first twelve weeks of the CDC, aside from suicide bombing the House Gods, the following forms of resistance were discussed: Cutting the ropes suspending the bridge, restarting the war by blocking the bridge from any potential sacrifice, and shooting flaming arrows across the canyon at the House Gods. They ultimately decided that the first two options wouldn't work, and would only be used as signs of a last-ditch, symbolic rebellion. There were skinny walkways leading to the river from both cliff sides, so cutting Harmony Crossing wouldn't actually keep anyone from reaching the other side. Moreover, the government officials, with aid from the rest of the residents, would forcefully remove them from barricading the bridge. While the flaming arrow option seemed more plausible, obtaining bows and arrows was as unlikely as making a bomb. But after the Steele's expulsion, ideas regarding resistance quickly became much more personal.

The discovery of Janet's conception led my wife to proclaim, "Coupling is killing. All members who wish to remain in our group must confirm now that they will never couple again."

All the members responded in the affirmative. And I stood there stunned as my wife declared the death of our foundation.

IX

Although the House Gods still seem to be in no rush to eat me, they are now at least steadily filling the field of grass at the end of Harmony Crossing. A Gothic House God, possibly the one that ate my son, is describing me as a beautiful animal, saying things like I bet he just has the tastiest toes. A small nautical House God shaped like a submarine with a periscope chimney seems to enjoy taunting me, asking if I'm happy being a helpless human, raised as a pug machine until my time of slaughter. I try to ignore the cacophony of the House Gods as I wait for them to call me forward. I pick my nose. I pee off the side of Harmony Crossing. I turn around and watch my unclothed wife watching me. I scan the House Gods for signs of goodness. But nothing works.

Exactly one-hundred days after the Steele's were expelled from the CDC, Katie gave birth to our final child, a beautiful girl, who we named Taylor. After the Deliverer left, my wife said, "The Collector will never take our daughter."

"What do you mean?" I asked.

"I mean what I said," she said, looking into our newborn's hazel eyes, "when the Collector comes, I'll tell him to back the fuck off. I'll tell him the Offspring Oasis will never collect this child."

We sat in silence, listening to our baby wail. Every few seconds, Katie tried to console our daughter with coos. I nibbled my fingernails until one of them bled. Eventually, I said, "What would that do to your Collective?"

"Goddammit, Kurt. Can't you just let me fantasize about keeping our baby for a bit? Can't you just let me imagine a world where we raise our child instead of handing her off to the city? Can't you just let me dream of having a family like our ancestors had before the fucking House God War?"

I nodded. I apologized. I tried to give her a hug, but she flinched. I wanted to tell her that one day we will be able to raise our family, that one day the Offspring Oasis, the Deck of Eligible Children, will no longer exist, but that fighting the city wouldn't bring this dream to fruition. I wanted to convince her that we had to work hand in wall with the House Gods to create a world where we could freely raise our family. But the anger in her eyes, the hurt in her heart, kept my mouth shut. She was far beyond words. She needed action, and I planned to show her what working with the walls could accomplish.

But where were the good House Gods?

Katie and I didn't talk much for the remainder of the month. She spent all her time with our daughter, and I spent most of mine at the Flaps of Fate searching for Devin Anderson but to no avail. When the Collector finally came, Katie handed Taylor over without a fight, her entire body fatigued with defeat. I tried to comfort her with my arms, but she pushed me away. We went to bed without words, our backs facing each other.

Tears stained my cheeks.

The day after the Collector took Taylor, I finally spotted Devin Anderson at the Flaps of Fate. The seat beside his was empty, and I practically sprinted to it.

"Hey, Devin," I said as I sat.

"Hello," he said, the last letter much louder than the rest as his face lit up with recognition. "Nice to see you again, Kurt."

"Where've you been?" I asked, and the dealer handed me my first pair—three of clubs and queen of hearts. "I've been here nearly every day looking for you."

"Been busy," he said.

I gave him a minute to elaborate, but he never did. The dealer turned the river, and we all showed our hands. I ended up winning with a full house, which I didn't even realize I had until the dealer pushed the pile of chips in my direction.

"I have some questions for you," I said, gathering my chips, "about what you said last time we shared a table."

"About the House Gods?" he asked, glowing.

I nodded. The other players around the table rolled their eyes or groaned or both. Apparently, they had already heard Devin's hypotheses about the House Gods and weren't looking forward to hearing them again. I received my second hand—two of diamonds and nine of clubs. I folded after the first bet was placed.

Devin asked, "Well, what would you like to know?"

"If not all House Gods eat people, well, then, what do they eat?"

"Furniture, of course," he said, like it was the most obvious fact in the world.

"I want to be clear," I said, "I believe you. I believe there are good House Gods. But how do you know? What proof do you have pertaining to their diets?"

He folded his hand. He grinned. He said, "The proof is in the logic."

"What the hell does that mean?" I asked, seriously doubting Devin for the first time.

"Think about the situation," he said, still smiling. "I've looked at it many different ways, and there is just no explaining how the massive House Gods could survive off one human sacrifice a day. Even if they divided the sacrifice up so that every House God could have an equal portion, a fingertip of a human being a day cannot possibly satisfy the stomach of a House God. And that's assuming they do share the sacrifice, which typically is not the case. House Gods swallow their sacrifices whole."

I envisioned my son walking into the open door of the Gothic House God. I saw him scraping away the curtains before disappearing inside forever. I tried to think of anything to counter Devin's claim, but I could not. Instead, I simply asked, "If only one House God eats one human a day, and the rest rely on furniture until it is their turn to feed on flesh, then why does a whole procession of House Gods make an appearance at every sacrifice?"

"It's simple, really," he said, sneaking a peek at his next hand. "House Gods aren't like us." He paused to call the bet and then paused some more.

"Obviously," I said, folding another shit hand.

"They don't have city-sponsored card games or coupling to consume their time. Sure, they can build more houses, but the more they build new beings, the less food they have. Instead of building new houses all day, diminishing their supply of furniture, they attend sacrifices to entertain them. Sacrifices are the closest thing they have to sport."

I nodded. All my doubts disappeared. Everything Devin said made sense to my mind. Sure, I wanted to believe him, I wanted some House Gods to truly be good, but my belief in this man was somehow deeper than desire. I kept on seeing good House Gods celebrating over a furniture feast, sharing couches and chairs, tables and toilets, all varying in size and color. I lost first that night, increasing my children's odds at being chosen from the Deck of Eligible Children, but I simply could not bring myself to care. I didn't even stick around long enough to see who the winner was, to know how many of my children's names would be replicated and how many times. Instead, I left the golden tent, dreaming of a future where my children would be my own.

After talking to Devin, my feet carried me home but my mind was elsewhere. Sure, Devin's sound logic convinced me, but would that be enough to convince the rest of the residents in the city? They all thought he was a lunatic after all. No, I needed hard proof, actual evidence that some House Gods were indeed good. But how?

And that's when it came to me, clear as a dream. Devin and I had to sneak across Harmony Crossing and explore the other side.

The plan: We would wait until dark. We would wait for a night when the moon was no more than a crescent sliver. I'd have no problem escaping my tent. My wife and I hadn't consensually cuddled since the Steeles' expulsion from the CDC three and a half months ago. I hugged her once a week or so, but she backed away every time. I had no idea what the Andersons' marriage was like, but I assumed it was better than mine. No matter, how Devin escaped wasn't my problem. We'd meet at the cliff side about one hundred yards north of Harmony Crossing. We'd head toward its base, but right before we reached it, we'd sneak down the path leading to the river. We'd swim across and climb up the other side. We'd wander around until the sun started its approach toward the horizon. We'd have one mission in mind: To find any evidence that would, without a doubt, prove some House Gods prayed for peace, too.

X

When I arrived at my tent, I stepped into the middle of a meeting of the CDC. I left the Flaps of Fate hours before this session started, and couldn't comprehend how I had walked for so long. I couldn't even recall where I had walked. I scooped a plateful of watermelon arugula salad from the serving bowl and sat at the table across from my wife. No one acknowledged me.

The Thompsons and the Ameses were presenting a wooden bow. It was the first bow anyone from the CDC had successfully constructed. Cassie Ames was demonstrating how it worked, pulling back the bowstring before letting it snap forward, causing the entire mechanism to reverberate. We were all mesmerized by the bow's music, and the second the string ceased shaking, the second silence tamed the tent, my wife asked her to do it again. Cassie obliged. And we listened to the bow music a minute more.

Once the bow had been returned to its

sheath, Katie asked, "And the bomb?"

The Simmonses, who had been in the CDC since its inception, along with a pair I had never seen before, who I came to know as the McCauleys, stood and presented a diagram on a large scroll. It took both Simmonses and Mrs. McCauley to keep the scroll unrolled— Mr. and Mrs. Simmons taking the top right and left corners, respectively, and Mrs. McCauley pinning the bottom against the floor. On the paper was a drawing of a large belt consisting of several different cylinders. The tops of the cylinders were open, and little squiggly lines were being distributed into each one.

"This," Mr. McCauley said, pointing to the belt with a stick, "is an explosive belt."

The members of the Collective "oohed" and "aahed" at the artwork.

Mr. McCauley continued, using his stick as a guide, "The belt is full of cylinders containing pipe bombs. Inside each pipe bomb, depicted by these lines here," he pointed to the squiggly lines, "are a variety of ball bearings, screws, nails, nuts, and any other form of shrapnel we can muster. When the bomber presses the button on the handheld device, connected to the belt through this wire, he or she will set off the explosive, sending the shrapnel in every direction, which will in turn tear apart the House God. This button must not be pressed until the sacrifice is inside the House God, otherwise there is no guarantee of lethality, understand?"

Everyone understood.

Katie said, "Great, Tom, excellent diagram. Now where's the bomb?"

"This process must not be rushed," he said.

"Of course, but what does that actually mean?"

"The prototype will be finished in a month or two."

"Two months for the fucking prototype?" Katie asked. Her voice, as it always was during CDC meetings, remained as calm as a candle.

"It's the best we can do with the supplies we have," Mr. McCauley said.

"I need this belt as soon as possible," Katie said. "We don't know how much time we're working with. One of our offspring could be chosen from the Deck of Eligible Children any day, and when that time comes, I want a successfully tested belt bomb on the waist of that parent. I want to burn the hungry House God fucker to the ground."

XI

Three months later, I finally spotted Devin Anderson again at the city-sponsored card games. I hadn't seen him since he had erased my doubts regarding the good House Gods, and I was excited to share my plan with him. I stood beside him at his table where he was one of three players remaining in the game, waiting for the hand to finish before I sat down. After the river, Devin decided to go all in, and one of the others at the table, Jill

Jones, called his bet. Devin was clearly bluffing because after Jill revealed her hand, he didn't even bother showing his. Instead, he wished her luck, stood up, and greeted me. I told him I had something of the utmost importance to impart, and he suggested we go for a walk.

Once we had left the tent, Devin headed north, away from the city, and I trailed him. I'd never been north of the Flaps of Fate, and I was anxious about being seen. Travelling outside the perimeter of the city, which was an oval looping around the Offspring Oasis and the tent we had just departed from, was strictly forbidden.

Devin must have noticed my nerves, because he insisted that we were perfectly safe, that he walked out here all the time, and that all the bedtime stories we heard in the Offspring Oasis of terrible monsters lurking outside of the city's limits were fabrications intended to instill fear with which the Coupling Caucus could seize more control. I asked him why the city would do this, and he said he wasn't entirely sure. But he hypothesized that no one alive today—not the average city resident, not the workers in the Offspring Oasis or the members of the Coupling Caucus—along with the mythical Mayor who leads them—had the slightest clue as to why they did what they do. He argued that centuries ago, during the time of the House God War, those who created these societal roles knew their importance and carried them out with purpose. But as our city evolved, as the city on the other side of the bridge evolved, our roles had stayed stagnant.

He said, "Now we execute our roles for a false sense of comfort. It's easier to live in a city where all we have to worry about is coupling for the cause than it is to live in a city where we have to worry about the responsibility of choice."

I opened my mouth and silence slipped out. I didn't know what to make of Devin's proclamations. His words certainly carried some weight, but why would those in the Coupling Caucus, why would the Mayor, continuously fulfill their role if they didn't believe it? It's obvious why the regular residents would observe their routine. Dissent carries severe consequences. But who could enforce punishment for dissent on the Mayor? Could comfort and fear truly be the sole sources keeping our city afloat? Can it be at all possible that the Coupling Caucus neither actively believes in their purpose nor has an ulterior motive?

"Lewis, my youngest son, is going to be sacrificed," Devin said, and his eyes became miniature waterfalls.

Instead of trying to convince him of how proud he should be, instead of wondering why he was acting like this, I wrapped my arms around this man and held him tight as he continued to cry. For the first time in my life, I was truly angry at the House Gods. Maybe my wife and her Collective were rubbing off on me, or maybe something from

Devin's speech had found a crevice in my subconscious. Whatever it was, I was more determined than ever to find the good House Gods.

I asked, "When will it take place?"

He cleared his throat. He said, "Two days shy of two months."

"Okay," I said, "I think I can help."

"Impossible," he said.

I ended our embrace and held his shoulders at arm's length. "Listen," I said, and his puffy eyes finally made contact with mine. "There's a reason I've been looking for you ever since we last met. I thought about the conversation we shared as I walked home that day, and honestly, I've been thinking about it practically non-stop ever since. I have a plan, and I think it might save your son."

"How?" he asked, looking at me as if I were some sort of messiah.

"Well, you are absolutely positive that there are good House Gods, right?"

"Yes," he said, almost before I had even finished asking the question.

"Then we must find them," I said, and I shared my plan with him.

When I was finished, Devin needed no convincing. He was immediately on board. His only question was when.

"For the past three months," I said, "I've been recording the size of the moon. If it follows a similar pattern, it should shine the least amount of light in eleven to thirteen days, and again in forty to forty-three days.

Which would you prefer?"

"I think we should go during both intervals," Devin said, his gloomy outburst fading fast. "We don't have much time before the sacrifice, and I think we should spend as much of it as we can on the other side of Harmony Crossing, scoping out the House God terrain and conspiring with the good ones on a plan to save my son."

I agreed. As we walked back toward the city limits, we made plans to meet just north of Harmony Crossing at midnight under the next new moon.

XII

Over a dozen House Gods have gathered on the grass and more are still coming through the trees. The largest is a white three-story neoclassical house with massive pillars lined across the front, stretching from its marble steps to its roof. The smallest is purple and shaped like an upside-down tea cup with a chimney curved like a handle. I look back at my wife, who is still holding her sign, and now a few more pairs from the Collateral Damage Collective have joined her, anxiously awaiting what I will do. They didn't bring signs, and the sun is becoming unbearable. My whole head feels like a boiling blister, and I'm beginning to care less and less what happens as long as it ends soon. But the houses keep coming. I have no idea when they will summon me, and I still can't bring myself to jump off Harmony Crossing. What if today is the day that the good House Gods make their presence known?

Katie and I, along with the rest of the CDC, were on a field trip. I had no idea where we were, but we had walked roughly four hours east outside of the city's perimeter. We were surrounded by darkness and dirt, and the only light came from the waning moon, less than half of which still shone in the sky. In just a few moments, Tom McCauley was going to blow up the belt.

He had presented the prototype to the CDC the day after I made plans to sneak across the bridge with Devin Anderson. Katie was thrilled, and immediately decided that the following meeting would last all night. They spent the entire evening discussing where to detonate the bomb, and for the first time since the Collective's inception, I made a suggestion.

I said, "The only possible place is miles outside of city limits."

Janine Mitchell questioned my contribution. She said, "What about the creatures that wait in the darkness?"

"There are creatures," I said, "but the ones you fear are fictional." I still didn't fully believe this. I'd only been outside of the city limits once and Devin and I didn't go far.

"How do you know?" Katie asked.

"Because," I lied, "I've explored the world outside of the city many times."

Everyone seemed impressed. For the first time, I was more than just misplaced mass to the CDC. I squirmed in my seat.

"Then it's decided," Katie said. "Next week, we walk east."

So we did.

Unlike the actual explosive belt, nobody was wearing this one. Tom McCauley held a switch sprouting a wire one-hundred yards long. When he flipped it, bright light illuminated the desert, and sand and shrapnel shot in every direction. The sound reminded me of childhood, of when I walked across model bridges in the Offspring Oasis with officials shouting at me from every direction. It was deafening.

Once the light had disappeared, everyone around me cheered. They slapped their hands together and hugged. They had successfully assembled a bomb that would one day blow one of them to bits.

"How long until we get the real thing, Tom?" Katie asked.

"We used almost everything we had for the prototype," Tom said. "Gathering enough supplies to make another explosive belt will likely take at least half a year, maybe longer."

Or, at least, I think that's what Tom said. My ears were still ringing.

"Let me know what you need," Katie said. "I'll do all that I'm able so you can construct another belt. Now that we've seen what this can do, none of us will be able to handle watching our offspring be sacrificed without one."

"I know," Tom said. "It's my sole priority."

"Good," Katie said.

We dragged ourselves back to the city and walked within its perimeter under the pre-dawn light. Everything was gray, and the air felt like static. As the sun kissed the horizon, I collapsed into bed.

XIII

I heard Devin approach in the darkness. I was waiting a little way down the path leading to the river so that only my head peeked out over the cliff side. He was looking for me. He was at least thirty minutes late.

When he walked past me, I hissed at him. He leapt.

"It's me," I said. "Down here."

He walked back toward Harmony Crossing until he found the path. A minute later he was standing beside me.

"You're late," I said, "and it's fucking freezing."

"I'm sorry," he said, shivering. "I woke my wife the first time I got out of bed, so I had to wait for her to fall back asleep. You know how it is."

I nodded. I doubted he could see me, but I didn't care. I didn't know how it was. Without another word, I walked down the cliff side and Devin followed. Going down was easy, the Harvesters still used the path every day, so the walkway was clear. It was what we would find at the bottom that I feared.

I hesitated when we reached the river. I had no desire to get wet in this weather, and if Devin wanted to have a chance at saving his son, he'd have to jump in first, which he did immediately. I clenched my teeth and dove in after him, dreaming about the good House Gods.

When I plunged past the surface, my entire body flexed. My ears instantly clogged and my brain felt like it was being impaled by icicles. It seemed like fingers of ice were prodding me, and every limb tingled as if it were pained with sleep. But no matter how hard I hacked at the water, they wouldn't wake up. I felt like an ice cube as I struggled to swim to the other side.

My hand came down on the dirt lip, and I promptly lifted myself onto land. My body shook, and my teeth continuously clapped. My clothes clung to my skin. The wind carried nails. I couldn't see Devin, so I quietly called his name, and he rested a hand on my head before sliding it down to my shoulder. I sighed. He asked if I were all right and I told him I was just fine. I trailed him to the cliff side, and we searched for the path. Weeds crawled over everything, but eventually Devin shrieked. He had found it.

This path's incline was steeper than ours, so we hoped the climb would be quicker. And it was at first, but about a third of the way up, we bumped into a problem. Due to time and inclement weather, rocks had slid down the hill and piled on top of each other. We stretched our hands above our heads, hoping to find the top of the barricade. I couldn't feel anything, and I was half a head taller than Devin, so I doubted he had any luck. But then I heard his feet leave the ground and his hands slap the rocks.

"Anything?" I asked.

"No," he said. "You try."

So I did.

And my fingers found a flat surface. I hung from the rocks for a moment before falling to my feet. I kneeled on my right knee and turned my left leg into a step, which Devin used to climb onto the rocks. A few seconds later, I listened to his feet land back on the path.

"The rocks don't go any higher?" I asked.

"No," he said, "not right here at least."

"Okay," I said, and I leapt, suspending from the top of the barrier.

It took me a minute to lift myself over the rocks, but once I had joined Devin again on the ground, the rest of the walkway didn't pose any problems. We reached the edge of the cliff side within minutes, and paused for a moment on the grass where the House Gods awaited their sacrifices.

I looked back at Harmony Crossing and imagined I was my son walking toward an open door. Had he ever played in the Green Room before? Did he even know what to call the last earthly surface he'd ever walk on? Back on our side of the bridge, grass only grew in the Green Room. But over here, grass appeared to grow everywhere, and I forgot how nice it felt beneath my feet. I slowly stepped toward the place where the Gothic House God's presence was, envisioned its black paint and maroon door, which creaked as it swung inward, asking me inside. My palms were wet and my body shook as I approached my son's killer, as I came closer to fulfilling little Kurt's purpose. I was only a step away, and as my foot came down beneath the House God's open frame, as I prepared for the eternal night, Devin's voice brought me back from my dream.

"Kurt," he was saying, "Kurt, let's go."

"I'm ready," I said, and I followed him past the sacrificial grounds and into the line of looming trees.

No human had been through these trees since the House God War, and I had no idea how high the chances were of being eaten. As the fear of being consumed without a sacrificial purpose settled in my mind, I nearly forgot about my wet clothes and the cold. We had almost arrived at the end of the stretch of trees.

Devin stopped at the last tree, and I followed his lead. We watched the House Gods for some time, and this was what we saw: Smaller House Gods were sloppily dancing on taller ones, in a few cases forming continually thinning towers, some House Gods were standing on their roofs, twitching occasionally but otherwise lifeless, while others were having a furniture orgy, which consisted of couches, chairs, and any other object not fastened to the ceiling or floor being spat from one House God's open window or door into another, this process endlessly repeating itself between a circular procession of buildings.

I had never seen any of these House Gods before, and when I asked Devin about it, he said he hadn't either. The ones at the bases of the towers were massive mansions varying in color and style, the largest of them being a blue colonial, a purple pueblo, and a white neoclassical. As the towers stretched skyward, there was everything from a small pink prairie to an elongated log cabin shaped like a dachshund. All the House Gods standing on their roofs were cottages, and most of them were of the German tradition. The House Gods playing with the furniture were just as varied as the ones composing the towers, though the most participatory were a black brick Italianate, a maroon Mediterranean, and a teal beach house with a sandpit for a porch.

"Do you think these are the good ones?" I asked.

"I don't know," he said, walking into the open, "but I'm going to find out."

"Wait," I called, "what if they eat you?"

"Then I die," Devin said, fearless, "but I have to try. If not, they are absolutely going to eat my son."

He continued his trek toward the House Gods, and I stayed behind the trees, waiting for a sign of goodness before I followed my friend. The House Gods continued dancing or feasting, too far gone in their respective reveries to notice that Devin was now halfway between them and the trees and increasingly getting closer. Even when he ascended the marble steps of the House God at the bottom of the biggest tower, the neoclassical mansion failed to acknowledge his weight. It wasn't until Devin knocked on the House God's glass door that everything stopped.

A cacophony of harsh whispers replaced the silence, each House God's sounds canceling any comprehension of the others' words. Then, just as quickly as it had begun, the space relapsed into silence. The glass door of the white mansion House God slowly swung inward, and Devin walked inside.

After the House God closed its glass door, after the creature had consumed my friend, the chaos continued. Those who were dancing danced some more, and those who were furniture feasting gorged again. The only House God who hadn't returned to its previous state was the one who swallowed my friend. The neoclassical mansion sat sincerely, as if it were contemplating the meal it had just finished, while those above it shook their walls like gelatin.

I cursed and kicked the grass. I paced back and forth, hidden by the trees, swearing as quickly as I could. I don't know how long I raged, but it wore me out. I trudged back through the trees and headed toward my tent.

When I reached Harmony Crossing, I didn't bother taking the long route. Instead, I walked right across it and wondered how Devin could be so dumb. Why would he so easily sacrifice himself to the House Gods if he wanted to save his son? I couldn't make sense of it. Sure, their scents are seductive, but they are only present once they open their door. Why would he run up to it and practically open it himself without any sort of plan? Why would my friend abandon our plan for peace?

I made it back to my city without any problems, and shortly after that I entered my tent. I got into bed and pulled the comforter over my head. I wanted more than anything to cuddle with my wife, but instead, I cried.

XIV

Two weeks after Devin's death, my wife made a gelatin dessert for the CDC. After I finished slurping some oysters, I covered my plate with the strange substance. I didn't eat any of it. I just repeatedly flicked it with my fingers, watching it dance. For the past two weeks, I'd been trying to avoid thinking of mine and Devin's disastrous adventure, but as I played with my dessert, I couldn't ignore it any longer.

Each time I touched the gelatin, each time it shook, I saw the tower of House Gods dancing above the white mansion as it savored my friend. Each time the gelatin danced, I bit my lower lip to keep my composure. I didn't want to make a scene.

On the other side of the tent, Tucker and

Millie Thompson were presenting a quiver full of arrows. They pulled a few out and passed them around. Tucker said the shafts were sculpted from the finest wood and the tips were made of steel. Once the members of the CDC had finished their examination, once the loose arrows had been returned to their quiver, my wife said they were all pleased with what they saw.

The Thompsons sat down, and Cassie and Gerald Ames stood up. Cassie revealed a bucketful of bows, pulling all of them out and handing one first to my wife, then to other members at random. There were ten in total, and those who held the bows simultaneously plucked the string, making the bows sing. After a few trial runs, they started to pluck their bows at different times, creating a harmonious rhythm. Despite the blues that had seeped into my blood, their bow song was beautiful.

But as they continued to make their music, I continued to flick my dessert.

At some point the meeting ended.

At some point the dark changed to dawn.

In the afternoon, I decided to take a trip to the Flaps of Fate. I hadn't played cards since Devin's consumption, and I don't exactly know what made me go that day. Maybe it was because of the bow music from the previous night, or maybe I just needed to escape my tent for a few hours. Either way, I went, and when I entered the tent, I was sure I had lost my mind.

Sitting at the first table and facing the tent flaps was Devin Anderson. He was waving at me. I blinked repeatedly. I slapped my cheek. I pinched my bicep until it bled. But no matter what I did, his ghost would not go away. I could not move.

He shoved all his chips into the pile and then promptly folded his hand. He got up from the table and approached. He asked if I would like to go on a walk. I nodded. What else could I do? I bit my lower lip as I followed the specter into the sun.

As we walked past the city's perimeter, he asked me where I had been. He said he had spent all day every day for the past two weeks waiting for me at that table. He told me he had something incredible to tell me.

"Okay, sure," I said. "Let's get it over with."

The excitement on his face was erased. "Is something wrong?" he asked.

"Is something wrong? Of course something's fucking wrong. You're dead. I saw it happen. I'm talking to a fucking ghost."

Devin laughed like a lunatic. I started to walk back toward the city. I couldn't tolerate my dead friend laughing at me like that.

"Wait," Devin said, regaining his composure.

"What now?" I asked.

"You said you saw me die, but you didn't. You saw me entering the mouth of a House God."

"What's the goddamn difference?"

"The difference is I'm alive, and I have so much to tell you."

"Alive?" I asked, awed.

"Yes, alive," he said, and he embraced me.

His flesh wasn't phantom; it didn't pass through me. His skin was warm. Somehow, Devin was not dead. I returned his embrace.

"How?" I asked as our hug came to its conclusion.

"When I left you in the trees, I didn't have much of a plan aside from exposing myself to the House Gods and tempting them to eat me. But after I knocked on the mansion's door, a strange sensation overcame me, and I knew where I was going to go, and I was okay with that. What I didn't know was that once I passed the threshold, nothing would change. I walked through the house as if guided by an invisible string until I reached its center and sat in a triangular room vacant except for a plush red chair. The walls and the ceiling and the carpet were red, too. And the second I felt comfortable in its chair, the House God spoke to me. Except it didn't speak with sounds. It communicated through mind-power."

Evidently, Devin was waiting for me to respond because he failed to go on. After a minute, I asked, "What'd the House God have to say?"

Devin cleared his throat. He said, "First, the House God assured me that no harm would come to me that night on their side of the bridge. It thanked me for coming because it had a message to share. This is more or less the message: 'Ever since I came into existence, I have never swallowed human flesh. Of course, I've swirled it around my mouth, as I am doing with you, but, as I always do, I'll soon spit you out.'"

"Wait," I said, "the House God has held humans within its door before? Are these people still alive? Are they preparing for peace as well?"

"I don't know," Devin admitted, and he sounded taken aback, as if he had yet to wonder who the humans were that had been inside this good House God. "I was too transfixed to ask. It told me that no House God built by the Founders had eaten a human. Instead, it said, 'we fill ourselves with furniture. But when the Founders discovered this untasteful tendency, they stopped building us. It took centuries, but we slowly learned how to create a passable House God. And as time continued its climb, the House Gods we built became bigger and better. The House Gods at the top of these towers are the products of our first success. As you move closer to the earth, you see the history of our aspirations. The House Gods directly above us are our most recent creations, and all the House Gods at the base of the towers were formed by the Founders.'"

"Did it say anything else?" I asked. "Anything about your son? Something like that?"

Devin nodded. He continued, speaking on the House God's behalf, "'We're almost done building the biggest House Gods yet. Once we complete them, we can proclaim war against the Founders and end the senseless slaughter of humankind. When we complete these astronomical mansions, the Founders will stand no chance despite outnumbering us five to one. Once that day comes, you will have nothing to fear, and we will save your son.' Then the House God spat me out. I never even mentioned my son to it. I didn't say anything, really. But the House God could sense my unease."

I didn't say anything.

Devin said, "Don't you know what this means? We were right, Kurt. There are good House Gods, and they will save us all."

"Next time we visit," I said, "I want to go inside the House God with you. I want to hear what the creature has to say." Even though I knew Devin wasn't lying, even though I knew some House Gods had to be good, I was skeptical. I had to experience this miraculous meeting myself.

XV

Two weeks later, my chance had finally come. Our second trip through the canyon was a little quicker than our first, and this time I didn't reenact my son's sacrifice on the other side. But aside from that, our trek to the House Gods was practically a replay. When we made it to the last line of trees and the House Gods came into view, even their actions seemed repetitive. The only significant difference between our last expedition and this one was that I joined Devin as he left the cover of the trees for an encounter with the white house.

As I took my first few steps into the open, I panicked. What if they didn't eat Devin last time because they wanted to use him as bait to lure more of his kind? What if they actually were good but they didn't like me? What if I were willingly walking into a trap?

As we wandered closer to the House God, I couldn't help but wonder what the repercussions would be if Devin and I were wrong. Would that mean that there are no good House Gods? Or worse, could we have been tricked by the bad ones while the good ones were off sleeping somewhere in the distance? If so, would there be anyone else on our side of the bridge capable of collaborating with the good House Goods to carry out a peaceful revolution? Or would my wife's way be the only way? Would the revolution require suicide belts and flaming arrows?

It wasn't until Devin pounded on the House God's glass door that all my worries withered. A blanket overcame and curled around my brain. I lost control of my body, and before I knew where I was going, I entered the House God.

I wasn't afraid. Somehow, the House God had communicated that I was completely safe, and no matter how hard I tried, I couldn't doubt it. On the other side of the entrance was an oval-shaped room with cerulean walls and a cerulean ceiling. Aside from the furnace across from the front door and the pair of blue chairs surrounding it, the room was vacant. Three doors lined the curved walls on either side of us, and without hesitation, we walked through the second door on our left. This led to a square green room whose floor was covered by a green rug with red kaleidoscopic patterns every few feet. Portraits of what must have been the Founding House Gods hung on the walls, and green chairs accompanied by gold lamps were scattered throughout. There was only one other door in this room, and it was on our right. It opened to a spiral ivory staircase covered with red carpet and supported by bronze railings. I was out of breath by the time we reached the mansion's second story, and we traveled through many more color-themed rooms before we finally reached the one Devin had told me about.

The red room was shaped like an upside-down triangle—a narrow doorway that opened to an increasingly wide space. A red couch had replaced the chair, and it stretched along the back wall. Once I sat beside my friend, the House God began to spread messages into our minds.

It silently said, "Devin, Kurt, I've been expecting you, and I'm so happy you have come."

Before I realized it, I thought, "How?"

I looked at Devin and he had tilted back his head, accentuating the lump on his neck as he narrowed his brow.

"Can they hear my thoughts?" I wondered, and as Devin nodded, an "oh shit" slipped across my consciousness.

The House God began to answer my initial question, saying something about how Devin had divulged my entire plan to it on his previous visit, but I struggled processing anything the house had to say. Instead, I involuntarily thought of all the things I never wanted anyone to know, which, consequently, shared all my secrets with Devin and the House God.

I thought about the first time Katie and I made love in the Green Room at the Offspring Oasis and how all our childhood training had vanished as I climaxed inside of this stranger who was soon to be my bride. I thought about the many years I loved Katie with more passion than was recommended by the Coupling Caucus. How I was enraptured by her, and how it all changed when little Kurt was sacrificed. How everything changed on a day that was supposed to symbolize the consecration of the success of our marriage. I thought about how as time passed, we became less like spouses and more like strangers sharing a small living space, except for when we fought about my reluctance about her Collective. I thought about the only affair I had ever had, which happened as I was leaving the Flaps of Fate one month after my wife founded the CDC. I was the first player at my table to lose that night, and the winner had over a dozen kids, which meant each of mine would appear in the Deck of Eligible Children a few times the following morning. As I exited the tent, Janet Steele recognized me and shared her losses, which were as equally as unfortunate. Maybe it was because of how my son's recent sacrifice had affected my wife and, given my performance that night, how I might be solely responsible for another of our offspring being sacrificed, or maybe it was because of mine and my wife's recent intimacy issues combined with the sudden and serious interest Janet had taken in me, but regardless of the reason, on our walk home that night, we hid behind my tent and pugged away our losses and our loneliness. I thought about the unbearable guilt I had experienced the following day, and how, two months later, the guilt grew when Janet Steele came to a CDC meeting with a slight baby bump.

But more than all of that, I thought about how proud I was as I saw my oldest son sacrifice himself, how I believed it was the best thing he could ever do. My cheeks burned as I helplessly admitted to Devin and the good House God that I had not only enjoyed watching my son walk into his death, but I had envied it.

"And I never want to have to watch my son do the same," Devin soundlessly said, relieving me of my rant, "which is why we need to come up with concrete plans to put a stop to the sacrifice system."

"The sacrifices must stop," the House God agreed, "but it must be the right time or else any progress we make will be easily reversed."

"But we don't have time," Devin said, "my son is going to die in fifteen days."

Again, the House God agreed, and I sat there absorbing their exchange without adding anything much like I had become accustomed to doing at CDC sessions.

"I propose," Devin said, shifting his gaze between me and the House God, confirming that he held our attention, "that in order to protect my son, the night before his sacrifice, you and all the other good House Gods sneak up on the meat-eaters as they sleep, and using the tools with which you build new creatures, you deconstruct the ones longing to lunch on Lewis."

I thought the plan seemed like a stretch, like it'd be impossible to pull off. My friend sounded desperate, and I felt embarrassed on his behalf. But just like before, the House God that held us within its walls did not deny Devin's request. Instead, it simply said, "Okay, so that's the plan."

Devin nodded. I felt uneasy about the plan. The future of our city's survival hinged on the good House Gods' reveal, or, in the case of Devin's newly announced strategy, on the deconstruction of the houses who regularly ate us. If any of the good House Gods made a sound as they approached, if they prematurely woke the bad ones from their slumber, they would be destroyed, and so would our city.

A minute passed, and I suddenly

remembered what Devin had said about other humans having previously been inside this House God's door. I asked our host if there were any truth to this claim.

"Certainly," the House God said, "but before you and Devin, I had not admitted a human within my walls for centuries. After the Founders built us, we were forced to feed on sacrifices. But, being morally opposed to swallowing human flesh, I, along with the Founders' other creations, would harbor the sacrifices inside of our walls until nightfall. When the darkness came, we spat them out of our front doors so they could return to their side of the bridge, and we satisfied our own hunger with furniture substitutes. Unfortunately, a human was summoned for sacrifice for the second time, and as she walked across the bridge, a Founder recognized her and deduced we hadn't been swallowing our offerings. Ever since that discovery nearly five hundred years ago, the Founders have been the only House Gods permitted to partake in the sacrificial ceremony."

"If only you could have been the House God waiting for Lewis on the other side of the bridge," Devin said, bringing the conversation back to his son, "you could have saved him no problem. But since that option ceased long ago, I still vote my original plan is the best way to proceed."

After the House God agreed again, it said the predawn light would be turning the black morning to static gray any moment. And without another word, Devin and I rose from the couch, and the same inexplicable sensation that led us into the red room led us back through the mansion and out its glass front door.

XVI

A week and a half had passed since Devin and I were inside of the good House God, and as I sat at the kitchen table with my wife, slurping some oysters, a fist pressed itself into the lining of our tent. Katie got up to unzip the flaps, and I brought my fist up to my mouth, chewing on my knuckles. How the hell could the city know what Devin and I had done? We had even climbed through the canyon on our return trip, and we were still under the cover of the black night.

As my wife reached the zipper, I shouted, "Wait."

"What?" Katie asked, her fingers resting on the metal sliver, her eyes spitting sparks.

I couldn't come up with a reasonable excuse, so I eventually just shrugged. Katie rolled her eyes. The entrance to our tent unzipped.

I let loose a shallow sigh as the Examiner stepped into our tent. But as he began to disrobe my wife, and I realized the reason for his existence, I began biting my fingers harder than I had before.

The Examiner poked and prodded my wife's bare belly with his right hand, taking a quick break every few jabs to jot down some notes on the pad of paper clutched in his left hand. This continued for an uncomfortable number of minutes until finally, with an exaggerated sigh, the Examiner exclaimed, "There appears to be an absence of a baby widening your womb. When this is the case, we perform an additional test, which, if you should fail, will place you and your husband on a six-month probationary period. During this time, you and your husband will be prohibited from visiting your children at the Offspring Oasis. At the end of the probationary period, we will return and re-administer these tests, and shall you fail a second time, you will be required to visit the Coupling Caucus to undergo fertility testing while your probationary period is extended indefinitely. Do you understand?"

"Yes," Katie said, tears strolling down her red cheeks.

"May I begin the second test?" the Examiner asked.

Katie nodded. What else could she do?

The Examiner examined the measurements on his notepad regarding the precise size of my wife's nodes. Once he knew what to expect, he pulled a ruler out of his robe and wrapped it around my wife's chest numerous times at varying angles. He scribbled a few short notes on his pad before moving on to the final part of the examination. He placed his hands on my wife's nodes, moving them in all sorts of directions as he gauged if they had grown.

"After my examination," the Examiner

said, "I can conclusively claim that you are without child. Therefore, you and your husband are sentenced to a six-month probationary period effective immediately."

My wife nodded. Even though she knew beforehand that this was the only possible outcome of the examination, her eyes were fixed on the Examiner, assaulting him with her stare.

"If I may," the Examiner inquired, "when was the last time you visited the Offspring Oasis?"

"Yesterday morning," I said.

"Well, I hope you had a pleasant visit, especially if it is to be the last."

Like his entrance, his departure lacked any type of salutation.

XVII

At the next CDC meeting, a few days following Katie's examination, there were two new pairs in attendance. I was unsurprised to see the Joneses enter our tent because we saw their youngest daughter was being sacrificed on our walk to our final Offspring Oasis visit. Whenever Katie and I visited our children, she would note what family was standing before Harmony Crossing, and almost without fail, the pair would appear at our tent the following meeting. Aside from the initial group, this was how she made her recruits. Consequently, there had never been two new pairs in the same month before, let alone a single night. But just before the session started, Devin and Anise Anderson stepped through our flaps.

When I first saw my friend and his wife, I told myself that they had come to share the news that the good House Gods had saved their son. They were here for celebration. But deep down, ever since Devin failed to report the revolutionary news the previous evening immediately after his son was scheduled for sacrifice, I knew the good House Gods never made an appearance. Seeing the Andersons here only further confirmed what a part of me already knew.

Their boy was dead.

As I processed this, Katie asked, "Who're you, and why're you here?"

The fear in her voice brought my mind back to our tent. I looked around the room, and each face mirrored the anxiety held within my wife's words except for the expressions of the Joneses. Since they themselves were new, they thought nothing about the Andersons' presence was odd.

"I'm Devin Anderson and this is my wife Anise. We're friends of Kurt."

Like anvils, all the eyes in the tent fell on me.

"Kurt?" Katie asked, clearly waiting for me to validate this man's accusations.

I gulped. "We're friends," I said, hoping that this conversation would miraculously conclude with that.

But of course, my wife continued, asking the newcomers, "How'd you hear about this meeting?"

To which Devin replied, "Kurt has told me all about the Collateral Damage Collective."

"Has he?" Katie asked, shocked.

I nodded.

"And how do you two know each other?"

"We met at the city-sponsored card games," I said.

"Is that all there is to the story?"

I shot Devin a stern glance, but he either didn't see it or didn't care because he said, "No, not at all. When we first met, I was sharing my conspiracy theories with the table about the good House Gods. I had become so accustomed to being ignored that I was getting ready to fold and move onto the next table when Kurt engaged me."

From there, Devin disclosed our entire friendship to the Collective. When he finished sharing our second trip to the other side of Harmony Crossing, he became silent.

Katie stared at me slack-jawed and speechless. The rest of her friends looked the same with the exception of the Joneses, who, unaware that this meeting was an anomaly, simply looked amused at the absurdity of the story, unsure whether or not they were supposed to actually believe it.

After a few minutes, Katie composed herself and said, "Is this true, Kurt?"

"Yes," I said, barely above a whisper. I cleared my throat. "Yes."

"Bullshit," Tom McCauley said.

I just shrugged. If Katie believed Tom over me, that'd make the rest of the evening a much easier experience. I couldn't imagine how they'd look at me all night knowing that I'd been inside of a House God and survived. But whatever the potential look was, I hated it.

"If there is one thing I can adamantly say about my husband, it's that when asked directly, he cannot lie. He can hide better than most, but when asked outright, he's unable to deceive."

"I repeat," Mr. McCauley said. "Bullshit."

"Say what you like," Katie said, "but if you disbelieve my husband, you disbelieve my judgement. And if you disbelieve my judgement, you're infinitely better off on your own than you are in my Collective. Just say the word and I'll unzip the flaps."

Either no one was brave enough to call my wife's bluff or she truly quelled their disbelief. Whatever it was, the CDC did not lose any members that night.

Katie once again directed her attention toward the Andersons. She asked, "If you have known about the CDC for quite some time, if you believe in the good House Gods, then why are you at this meeting? Surely you know what we aim to accomplish."

"We are aware," Anise said, breaking her silence for the first time since she arrived. "And to be clear, I never believed good House Gods existed. But I was also unaware that the Collateral Damage Collective existed before last night. Because despite the plans our husbands had made with the House Gods, despite their belief, the good still allowed the bad to consume my son. Consequently, after the sacrifice, Devin confessed the failed plan to me and offered up a much better ulterior." She opened her arms, signaling the CDC. "You see, while it's too late for Lewis, it might not be too late for our other offspring, and it might not be too late for yours. We are here tonight because we want to destroy the House Gods once and for all."

"And what about you, Devin," Katie said, "do you share the same sentiments as your wife?"

"Ever since I saw my son's sacrifice, I've wanted nothing more than to watch all the House Gods burn."

"Good," Katie said. "I was hoping to hear that. And to that end, I think I might have some good news for you. Tonight, the Thompsons and the Ameses are going to update us on their bow and arrow collection. But before we get into all that, I insist we take a brief break and get some refreshments."

During the intermission, no one spoke. Everyone was too busy digesting what they'd just heard, praise be to the House Gods. I loathed the idea of talking to Devin the traitor. And yet, despite his betrayal, despite losing my only confidant and, more importantly, friend, I couldn't despise him for it. After all, the House God had broken its promise to him at the expense of his son's life. When it came right down to it, what else should he have done? Still, I don't think I would have abandoned our cause if I were in his shoes. But I also don't expect him to react as I would. I had been married to Katie far too long to expect like-minded people to react to the same situation singularly. I just wished all of this were easier.

After the break, Katie had the Joneses introduce themselves. It only took a minute. They said what every other pair said during their introduction except for the Andersons. They said that their child was sacrificed and that they will no longer create offspring for the House Gods' consumption.

After the introduction, the Thompsons and the Ameses spoke about their bow and arrow collection's growth. Like every update, it was bigger but not nearly big enough yet to attack the House Gods. Like every week, I resumed my role as the mass sitting beside the woman in charge.

After the meeting, Devin and Anise left without acknowledging my existence. However, they took the time to shake my wife's hand as she sat across the table from me.

After the last guest had gone, Katie eyed me longingly from across the table. It was the first time she had looked at me this way since she had banned all members of the CDC from engaging in any form of intercourse. I returned the look, expecting her to realize what she was doing and end it, but she did not. It felt like minutes had passed since either of us last blinked. But eventually, she broke the connection and smiled.

She asked, "Kurt, why didn't you ever tell me what you and Devin were doing?"

I shrugged. I couldn't think of anything to say. Her reaction had me speechless.

"Were you that afraid?"

"Yes," I said, my voice coming back full force, "but it wasn't what you think. I wasn't scared that you'd be angry or hate me or anything like that. These days, I could deal with that."

"You could?" Her slight frown surprised me.

"I think so," I said. "Sorry."

She shook her head, knocking my apology aside. "What, then?"

"Mostly, I was terrified that you'd ask me to stop. If you did, if you do, I don't know if I'll be able to keep on trying to work with the good House Gods. And if that were to happen, I'm afraid of resenting you for it."

"So you do still believe some of them are actually good?" she asked, incredulous. "Despite Devin having come to his senses?"

"I do," I said. I added, "My belief in their goodness is as strong as my belief in their existence."

"I see," she said, shaking the disappointment out of her mind. "Of course, I disagree. And, to tell you the truth, I think you're an idiot. But Kurt, I am proud of you, too." She smiled once more, and the look of longing returned.

She reached across the table and took my hand in hers. She rose to her feet and led me past the hanging curtain to our bedroom where she disrobed and rested atop the comforter. My eyes widened and my plank stiffened as I removed my own robe.

We didn't couple. We didn't even kiss. Instead, we pressed our flesh against one another, absorbing each other's warmth. I wished this moment would stretch into eternity, that sleep or sounds would never move our minds away from each other. But no matter how bad I wanted it, a looming thought ebbed at my elation, which, long after our body heat had caused us to sweat, brought my wife to ask what was wrong.

"It's just," I said, cursing my curiosity, "I'm wondering why my plans for peace have made you proud."

Despite trying to contain it, despite keeping her lips sealed shut, she laughed. It came through her nostrils. Katie quickly silenced herself as she covered her nose with her hand. She breathed deep. She said, "Isn't it obvious?"

I shook my head, her laughter still reverberating around my skull.

"Until a few hours ago, I believed watching our son die had left you unaffected. Worse, I thought you took pride in having witnessed it. And I thought you prayed more of our children would be selected for sacrifice. Never before have I been so happy to be so wrong, and I was wrong, wasn't I?"

"Yes," I said, nodding, "you were." I didn't tell her that she wasn't always wrong about this. It's a shortcoming that I still struggle admitting to myself.

"You idiot," she said, smiling. "I'm proud because you're taking action against the House Gods. I'm proud because you're resisting the Coupling Caucus. I'm proud because you're fighting for our family, albeit, in your own strange way. Kurt, after all these years, I'm proud to call you my husband again."

I kissed Katie on the forehead. Neither of us said anything more, and my wife soon sifted into sleep.

Hours after Katie had started to snore, my thoughts turned to Devin. I hoped the CDC session was just a dream, and that in the morning, I'd awake to find he was still my friend. But as the light slowly grew outside our tent, dispersing the darkness, the dream didn't end. As Katie opened her eyes, stretching her arms above her head, I would not wake up.

XVIII

The good House Gods waiting on the other side of Harmony Crossing now nearly equal the bad. The purple pueblo stands on the outskirts of the congregation, and beside it, the blue colonial. Near the Gothic House God by the base of the bridge waits the pink prairie. In the center of the House God gathering stands the dachshund-shaped log cabin. Most of the House Gods who formed the night towers are present. At least fifty good House Gods are here. Could this be the day that we actually achieve peace? Could everything I've been fighting for finally come to fruition? I can't tell. I'm distracted by the state of my skin. My head throbs, and when I stroke my legs, my pores feel like sandpaper. Despite the heat, despite the full-body burn, I can't find a single drop of sweat on my body. Come to think of it, I can't even remember how long it has been since I last perspired. I suddenly start dry heaving, and my whole body shakes uncontrollably. Is this what dying feels like? My tongue tastes like dirt. My vision hovers above my body. The scents of peppermint and gingerbread, of campfires and cedar, dismantle my will and dictate my desires. I lie flat on my back on Harmony Crossing and convulse, but all I want is to follow the alluring aroma. As I send ripples through the bridge, I hear the House Gods' call. Sounding like a mechanical choir, they sing:

"All hail the House Gods."

Six weeks after Devin and Anise joined the CDC, I snuck across the canyon to visit the good House Gods. I had failed to visit them during the previous new moon, two weeks after the sacrifice of Devin's son. I feared that their reason for refusing to show up at Lewis Anderson's summons wouldn't be sufficient. What if their justification for their broken agreement were cowardice or apathy? How could we continue to work harmoniously for peace if we didn't share the same values? But by the time the second new moon had rolled around, I had dispelled the hypothetical dissonance and decided to speak to the good House Gods about what had gone wrong.

The trek through the canyon didn't pose any problems, and when I had surpassed the last line of trees between myself and the House Gods, I discovered that they were dancing and feasting just as they had done during both of my visits with Devin. I approached the white neoclassical House God and climbed its marble steps. The instant my knuckles knocked against its glass door, it swung inward and its intoxicating scents pulled me inside. A few minutes later, I was in the heart of the house, sitting in the lone red chair occupying the red room. The couch I had shared with Devin had seemingly disappeared.

"Welcome back," the House God said without sound. "Last month you were missed."

I nodded. "It's good to be back."

"Is it?" the House God asked. But before I could respond, it went on, "I was worried you wouldn't come again after we let Devin's son die. And I assume it's no coincidence that you've come alone."

"No," I said, "it's not. And that's why I couldn't come last month, and why I had to come tonight. I mean, I guess what I'm trying to say is, why did you let him die? Did you not agree to Devin's plan? Did you not say that you and your companions would disassemble the bad House Gods the night before the sacrifice?"

"I did," said the House God.

"Then why didn't you?" I asked.

"For one thing, the plan was terrible. As Devin shared it, even you thought it was futile, did you not?"

I nodded. I wondered how the House God knew.

"Because you thought it at the time, and consequently, you spoke it. Devin couldn't hear the thought though because he was too focused on his schemes."

"But if you had no intention of following his plan," I said, "then why did you agree to it at all? Why didn't you just tell him it was an impossible plot?"

"Because there was no plan that could have saved his son," the House God said. "Devin's boy was destined to die, and telling him as much wouldn't have softened the blow. If there is no way to change the future, is it not better to hold onto hope, no matter how false, than it is to wallow in misery while it can be avoided?"

"I don't know," I admitted.

"Would Devin have benefitted from an additional twenty-four hours of misery?"

Again, I said, "I don't know." I added, "But if you hadn't lied, at least he wouldn't have felt betrayed."

"He'd have felt betrayed either way," the House God said. "He knew his son was going to die and he believed we were the only ones who could have stopped it. If we told him we wouldn't, he would've felt just as betrayed as he feels now."

"Maybe," I conceded, "but why wouldn't you make an appearance at the bridge to save his son?"

"The timing wasn't right," the House God said, as if it were the most obvious statement ever made.

"What does that even mean?" I asked, annoyed.

"If we had confronted the House Gods at the bridge as they waited to summon their sacrifice, they would have demolished us. Not only would the boy still have been swallowed, but any possible chance of creating future peace would have been devoured as well."

"I see," I said, and I couldn't think of anything else to say.

After a few moments of thoughtless silence, the House God said, "It's getting late, and I still have some dancing to do."

Before I was aware of any movement, my body had carried me out of the red room and down the arched corridor. As I walked down the spiral staircase, the House God added, "Will I see you on the night of the next new moon?"

"You will," I said, stepping out its front

door.

XIX

A month and a half later, nearly one hundred days since Katie and I had seen our kids, she said to the members of the CDC, "Janet Steele is dead, and with her death dies our chances of suicide bombing a House God if one of our children is ever chosen."

"Janet's dead?" I said, and a strange sort of sickness filled my stomach.

"What's it matter to you?" Katie asked.

I just shook my head. Janet's death didn't matter to me. But its connection to the bomb worried me for some reason.

"What are you talking about, Katie?" Tom McCauley asked, who was weeks away from completing a useable suicide belt for the CDC.

"It happened yesterday," Katie said. "Jill Jones visited my tent last night and informed me. Jill, will you fill everyone in?"

I regretted playing cards at the Flaps of Fate last night, and not just because I was the first to lose. Missing Jill's visit and consequently being put off guard before my wife's Collective caused my skin to flare.

Jill Jones stood and said, "John and I were walking back from seeing our children at the Offspring Oasis when we heard the explosion. When we reached the bridge, smoke still hovered over the grass on the other side. The Coupling Caucus had already arrived and were interrogating Jordan Steele. He admitted he and his wife had built the belt at home alone just in case any of their children were chosen for sacrifice. Their plan was to volunteer to walk with the child. When their newborn was selected from the Deck of Eligible Children, they had the perfect reason for volunteering because Nancy Steele was too young to walk. So Janet put the belt around her waist, picked up their baby girl in her arms, and walked across Harmony Crossing."

"Did they blow up the House God?" asked Anise Anderson, excited.

"That's the worst part," Jill said. "The newborn must have pressed the button or done something to her mother to cause her to hit it prematurely because the belt blew up the moment they stepped off Harmony Crossing, long before they reached the hungry House God. The Coupling Caucus apologized to the House God profusely for the delay in its meal, and then they forced Jordan to sacrifice himself in his blown-up newborn's place."

Jill sat back down, and I repeated the name Nancy over and over again in my head as if it were a sweet that I refused to swallow. Nancy, my youngest child. Nancy, the one neither my wife nor I would ever know. Nancy, the one who was sacrificed before she could even walk. Did she have any clue as to what was about to happen when the belt blew? Did being torn apart by shrapnel hurt? Nancy, how bad did you hurt?

Katie's voice took charge of the room once

more. She was saying, "The Coupling Caucus has since outlawed clothing from being worn to sacrifices. I stopped by the bridge this afternoon to confirm, and the parents who were watching their child walk across had indeed left their robes at home for the occasion. So unless someone knows of a way to make the suicide belt invisible, it's no longer of any use to us."

"Housepugger," Tom McCauley said under his breath, "all that work and for nothing. Our children are defenseless."

The next morning, I rose with the sun, threw on my robe, and brewed a powerful pot of coffee. The second it was ready, I left the tent with the whole pot in hand and went for a long walk north. By the time I had reached the Flaps of Fate, the coffee had cooled enough so that it wouldn't scald my tongue, and I took a big swig while I walked. My pace slowed significantly once I had surpassed the city's perimeter, but I pushed onward.

Once I was far enough away from the city, I repeatedly replayed the CDC meeting in my mind, except I forced myself to forget about Nancy for the time being. Mourning the loss of a child I never knew, even if she was my own, would only interfere with my ability to plan for future peace. Mourning Nancy would have to come later.

For now, the good House Gods and I were incredibly lucky that Janet had botched the suicide bombing attempt. If she had pulled it off, the House God War would have no doubt resumed immediately and our entire city would have easily been eradicated. Her failed attempt also bought the good House Gods and I a little more time to overthrow the current sacrifice system because it destroyed the CDC's own hopes at a suicide mission, but we would have to act fast. Katie and her Collective were now more determined than ever to avenge their dead children. It was only a matter of months before they possessed what they believed to be an adequate supply of bows and arrows and resumed the war.

The only viable option left was to create a new plan and peace treaty to present to the good House Gods under the next new moon. This was my new plan: All the good House Gods must make an appearance at a forthcoming sacrifice. They would express their desires for peace with humanity and present them with the new treaty, which would demand equal treatment between House Gods and humans. Of course, the Founders would find this absurd. But then the good House Gods would explain how they had been working alongside the humans at night, and how the humans had created weaponry far beyond anything seen before. They would tell the Founders that humankind would rather live together in harmony with the House Gods as opposed to being forced to obliterate them. But if the House Gods refused to put an end to the sacrifice system, they would be leaving the humans with no other option.

The success of this plan hinged on the good House Gods' ability to bluff. If there was one thing I learned from the city-sponsored card games, it was that the best bluffer had the highest odds at excluding their offspring's names from appearing in the Deck of Eligible Children the following day.

Admittedly, this plan was a long shot and a huge risk. If the Founders called the good House God's bluff, we would lose all hope of peace. But if we didn't do anything, we would lose everything all the same. Time was running out, and this was our best bet. Now I just had to convince the good House Gods to play along.

XX

Under the following new moon, two weeks after I devised my new peace treaty, my whole body quaked as I made the trek from the trees to the white neoclassical House God. Of course, I was excited to share my new plan, but what if the House God thought it was crap? And if it did, would the white house even tell me, or would it lead me on like it had Devin? When I reached the top of its marble staircase, the glass door swung open before I had even knocked. I gulped. Its alluring aroma soothed my nerves some, but not enough to suppress my shaking. I inhaled its intoxicating scent deeply as it led me past the oval-shaped cerulean room, through the green one, and up its ivory stairs, but even as I entered the red room and sat in its single chair, my anxiety still lingered.

"What can you possibly be so afraid of?" the House God asked. Apparently, it was the first thought that had crossed its mind.

Even if I wanted to prolong the presentation of my plan, I could not. The House God's question combined with my unease had kept it on the forefront of my mind. Consequently, I divulged the entirety of my new peace treaty without taking a single breath.

When I had finished, the House God said, "Clearly, that could never work."

Instead of further defending my idea, the House God's deadpan dismissal had caused me to ask, "And why not?" I wasn't even sure if I wanted to hear its answer.

"For a few reasons," the House God said. Ignoring my indecisive thoughts, it went on, "First, the Founders would never buy the bluff. Even if they thought we believed the weapons existed, they would chalk it up to us being less intelligent than they, and consequently, your bluff had simply fooled us. The Founders believe humans are far too inferior to create a weapon that could inflict the slightest amount of damage upon them. After all, your ancestors went to war with them and failed to kill a single House God.

Second, if by some miracle the Founders did buy the bluff, would the humans actually accept their peace offering with open arms? The slightest dissent on the part of your people would start the war all over again."

I thought about my wife's Collective, and how they would demand the destruction of all the House Gods who partook in the sacrifices before accepting the offering of peace, and in doing so, I unintentionally confirmed the neoclassical House God's claims.

"Ultimately though," the House God said, "the only way to achieve our aims has nothing to do with the humans or any peace treaty that you concoct. It doesn't even have anything to do with the Founders. A true and long-term peace agreement solely depends on the astronomical mansions my companions and I are in the process of constructing."

"What makes you so sure these astronomical mansions are the key?" I asked.

"Their size, primarily. The three mansions we are building will each be as large as the tower of houses dancing above me. They will practically scrape the sky. Once these astronomical mansions are complete, we will present them to the Founders as they gather at a sacrifice and demand that they let the human waiting on the bridge return to its tent unharmed. Then we will present them with two options. They can either forego human flesh for the rest of their days, or they can crumble under the might of our massive creations. They will choose the former, of course. For as much as they enjoy the taste of humankind, they care more about preserving their walls. Once the Founders have consented to peaceful cohabitation, presenting the astronomical mansions to the humans will show those who want revenge against the House Gods just how useless their resistance will be. Both the Founders and the humans will, essentially, be forced to live harmoniously hand in wall."

"How long until these House Gods will be built?"

"That's the problem," the House God admitted. "We have run into some logistical issues."

"What kind of logistical issues?" I asked.

"We are short on supplies," the House God said, matter-of-fact. "In the beginning, many of our original creations volunteered their materials to the astronomical mansions, and as the projects grew, some who were hesitant at first also donated their walls. But now that each creation is only a single-story shy of completion, we have run out of House Gods willing to sacrifice their existence for the cause. That's why we were unable to save Devin's son, and why we won't be able to bring about peace for the foreseeable future."

"Are you fucking kidding me?" I asked. I didn't mean to swear at it or sound upset, but I couldn't keep my thoughts under control. "If you're that close, why don't you just dismantle one of your earlier House Gods against their will to complete the mansions?"

"The materials must come from a volunteer," the House God said. "If we were to deconstruct a House God against its will, we would be doing the very thing we are fighting against."

"But at what cost?" I asked. "What if a thousand more children die before another House God decides to be deconstructed?"

"Then so be it. Dozens of House Gods have already sacrificed themselves to save your species because we believe it is right. We do not benefit by this, nor do we need to do it. But when the next House God is ready, and only when it is ready, we will immediately salvage its walls and complete the mansions."

"Fine," I said, breathing deeply. "Then why don't you just build two astronomical mansions? Or make them a tad smaller than originally intended?"

"If only we could," the House God said, sighing. "But in order to get the Founders to surrender, the House Gods we are building must fit the original blueprints. Otherwise, the Founders will be able to overcome them, and despite the losses they would suffer in the process, they would eventually demolish the astronomical mansions, and with them, any chance of peace. Unlike humans, House Gods are, by nature, logical beings. If the Founders calculate that they cannot win, they will not fight."

"Okay," I said, "so what do we do now?"

The neoclassical House God said, "Now, we wait."

XXI

Five months into our probationary period, Katie and I sat on opposite ends of our kitchen table as the Thompsons and the Ameses updated the CDC on their bow and arrow operation. They kept on pulling bows out of burlap sacks and passing them around the tent. Each time they reached back into a bag for another bow, my heart sunk a little lower, and the number of days the good House God's had to finish their mansions diminished.

Katie kicked my leg under the table, and I shifted my focus to her. She was scowling at me, and it took me a moment to realize I had been absentmindedly slurping my oyster soup. I set my spoon down in the bowl and returned to the distribution of bows, but the bags were finally empty.

Nearly everyone in the CDC held a bow in their hands, and Cassie Ames assured us they had just as many quivers full of arrows back at her tent. As everyone plucked their respective strings, the bow music had lost its beauty. However, Katie looked pleased, and I nervously returned to my soup, fearing they were just weeks away from carrying out their plan to attack the House Gods.

At last, Katie asked how long it would be before the bows were ready for action.

"Five and a half months," Tucker Thompson said, "at most."

"Excellent," Katie said, smiling.

I smiled, too. The good House Gods should have at least one-hundred and fifty days to save our city.

Exactly six months after Katie and I were put on probation, the Examiner returned to our tent. Like before, he failed to greet us as he stepped inside, and he immediately disrobed my wife. He spent much less time squeezing her stomach and neglected to write anything in his notepad.

Before he moved onto my wife's nodes, he asked, "Have you been coupling?"

Katie stayed silent, so I said, "Of course."

"Twice a day as recommended by the Coupling Caucus?"

I lied again, and Katie's eyes burned like a crematory into which she seemingly wanted me to climb.

"Very well," the Examiner said. "Then I will move onto the final portion of the examination."

As he had done during his last visit, he studied the measurements on his notepad detailing the expected size of my wife's nodes. Once he believed he knew what size he should find, he took various measurements before feeling them for himself.

"It's as I expected," the Examiner explained, "you, Katie Nolan, are not carrying a child within your womb. Because you and your husband claim to be coupling, you must visit the office of the Coupling Caucus located deep within the Offspring Oasis to test both of your fertility. Your mandatory appointment is scheduled for tomorrow at dawn. Failure to show up will result in severe consequences. There are no adequate excuses for missing this appointment. Do you understand?"

"Yes," Katie said, "we understand."

"You may refurnish yourself with your robe if you wish," the Examiner said. And with that, he left us alone in our tent.

With her robe still scrunched around her ankles and tears staining her cheeks, Katie said, "We are absolutely not attending that fertility test tomorrow, and there is nothing you can say to change my mind."

"I know," I said. I didn't even know if I wanted to go. I mean, what difference could it possibly make? Katie's Collective would declare war against the House Gods in three and a half months, and unless the good ones had completed the construction of their three mansions, nothing could stop the CDC. The fertility tests were futile.

It had been a few days since we failed to appear at the fertility test, and we had yet to hear from the Coupling Caucus. As the day turned to dusk, Katie continued pacing back and forth before our tent flaps as she had done the previous few days, anxiously awaiting the city's decree.

"Do you think they'll summon me for sacrifice?" Katie asked, eyes gleaming. "Is forgoing the fertility test enough?"

"I don't know," I shrugged. I didn't understand why Katie was so intent on being sacrificed since her suicide belt was no longer an option.

But when the knock finally came, she squeaked. She unzipped the tent before the official could even return his hand to his side. When I looked to see who it was, I saw the massive man standing outside our tent. Like on his last visit, in which he delivered the letter condemning our son to death, he handed an envelope to my wife and left without speaking. Before he had taken five steps, the tent had zipped shut again.

When Katie read who the letter was addressed to, her jaw dropped. "This has to be some kind of mistake," she said, shaking her head.

"What?" I asked, fearing maybe another of our offspring were to be sacrificed for Katie's refusal to reproduce.

"The letter is addressed to you," Katie said.

My stomach swirled. The room seemed to spin. I dry heaved. "Are you sure?"

She held out the envelope for me to see. Sure enough, *Kurt Nolan* were the only words written on it. Katie broke the seal and began to remove the letter.

"Don't open it," I said, practically screaming.

"Why not?" Katie asked, pausing mid-extraction.

"Because it's addressed to me," I said.

Katie held it in her hands for a moment before slowly pulling the letter all the way out.

"Give me the goddamn letter," I said.

"For the love of the House Gods," Katie said, thrusting the letter into my hand. "Calm down."

I began to read the letter, but before I finished the first phrase, Katie interrupted. She said, "Aren't you going to read it out loud?"

"Fine," I said, and I began to read my fate aloud. This was what I read:

Because of you and your spouse's failure to produce a child this year, compounded by your refusal or inability to undergo fertility testing, you, Kurt Nolan, are summoned for sacrifice in eighty-one days. Since you have established a history of missing mandated appointments, we want you to note that should you fail to be on Harmony Crossing at dawn on the eighty-first day from today, the Repossesser will personally escort your broken body to the bridge. In advance, we thank you for your continued service to our city.

With gratitude,
The Coupling Caucus

My insides crumbled, but somehow my body remained upright. Katie, however, had regained her grin. I asked her about its existence.

"Because," she said, speaking through her smile, "this is the kind of break the CDC has been waiting for. A perfect opportunity."

"My death is not an opportunity for your Collective, Katie."

"Of course not," Katie agreed. Her smile vanished suddenly, and she wrapped her arms around my bicep. "Surely you don't think I'm celebrating your death, do you, Kurt?"

"I most definitely do," I said, confident she could not spin what had just come from her mouth.

"What use could you possibly be to us if you were killed?" she asked, sincere. "Even you must see that there is no benefit in that?"

I didn't know how to respond. I decided to shrug.

"The opportunity the CDC has been waiting for," Katie said, releasing my arm, "the one that you can bring, is symbolic, public resistance. All you have to do, Kurt, is remain in our tent. And don't worry about the Repossesser," Katie added, "the CDC will band together to keep you away from any harm."

This sounded too easy, and I waited for the catch, but it never came. Eventually, I said, "I'm sorry, Katie, but I don't think I can let you and the CDC do that."

"And why not?" Katie asked. Despite her

tone staying the same, her flesh became slightly flushed.

I cleared my throat. "The Coupling Caucus has control over all our offspring. Over all the children created by your comrades in the CDC. What do you think the consequences will be of this act of minor resistance? I simply cannot risk the lives of the rest of our children by abstaining from sacrifice. If our children are to survive, the resistance must be done through peace or it must not happen at all. But if that moment doesn't come before my summons, then I will be at the bridge and I will sacrifice myself to the House Gods, at the very least, for the sake of our children."

Katie refused to refute my reasoning. Instead, all she said was, "We'll see about that, Kurt. We shall see."

Skipping dinner, my wife went to sleep. I made myself a small bowl of oyster soup, wondering whether or not her decision to refrain from a debate favored me or her.

XXII

Katie started the next CDC session with this statement: "All of our abstaining has finally conceived a consequence. Two days ago, my husband and I received a letter summoning Kurt to be sacrificed. This is the moment we have all been awaiting. Now that we know what our covenant of celibacy is capable of, more and more members will receive their summons in due time. And let me be clear: Each appointed sacrifice will point to a day of fasting for the hungry House Gods."

I rolled my eyes. My wife winked at the Thompsons and the Simmonses, who would be the next pairs to receive the letter because they had their last child only one month after Katie gave birth to Taylor. Of course, they would be the first pairs to actually resist the sacrifice because I certainly wasn't going to skip it. Not that it would make any difference. There was no way the city would allow a day to pass without a sacrifice. Even if the CDC managed to hold off the Repossesser, the city would just send a child or two in the original sacrifice's place.

"So Kurt," Devin said, and all the eyes in the room turned to me, searing my skin with their intensity, "are you excited to be the emblem of the Collective's first public act of resistance?"

As Devin spoke, he looked through me, and I knew this was no longer the man who was once my sole friend. I shook my head slightly. I shrugged. I couldn't figure out how to put my thoughts into words, but I was nowhere near excited.

"He believes he will attend the sacrifice," Katie said. "He has refused to resist."

"Is that so?" Anise asked, looking into my eyes.

"It is," I said, regaining my voice. "When the time comes, I will be on Harmony Crossing. When the House Gods summon me, I will heed their call. I do not see any value in resistance."

"If he refuses to resist," Tom McCauley said, grinning, "then we must make him by any means necessary, right Katie?"

"If he continues to refuse," Katie said, "then we will remove his choice. We will tie him up and hold him hostage until the day of his sacrifice has passed."

My stomach dropped. I bit the inside of my lip until I tasted blood, until the pain of raw flesh convinced me of the reality of my wife's words. But how could this be my wife? My Katie? I swallowed the blood. I said, "You'll have to kill me if you want to keep me away from my sacrifice." I didn't mean it. But I couldn't think of anything else to say.

"Gladly," Mr. McCauley said, and his grin grew.

"We won't kill you, Kurt," Katie said in a soothing voice, though it failed to achieve its desired effect. "You don't have to worry about that. I could never hurt you permanently. The most we would do is knock you unconscious if you compel us to. But trust me when I say I would hate to do that, and I hope you don't force us to resort to such violence."

My body crumbled to sand, and my mind rolled through the tent in waves. I dry-heaved. Then I actually vomited all over the kitchen table. My regurgitated oyster soup blended with whatever unconsumed portion was left in my bowl. Katie didn't move. She looked into my eyes. My wife told me to get everything out now, to do whatever it was I needed to do to realize that I would resist, because in seventy-nine days, I would refuse to be on Harmony Crossing.

I succumbed to her wishes with a nod. Surrounded by her Collective, continuing to oppose her hopes seemed useless. Katie smiled, but I did not return the gesture. I had lied to my wife without using words.

The next new moon had arrived, and I was sitting on the white neoclassical House God's red chair. I was silently saying, "In two months' time, I will be summoned for sacrifice. So if the astronomical mansions are not completed by then, I will no longer be able to coax my people to accept the promise of peace when it comes." I didn't mean to make it sound like a threat.

The House God said, "I will inform the others, and we will all reevaluate our willingness to donate our walls to the cause."

"Thank you," I said, "but my life should be the least important reason a good House God gives up theirs. My wife and her collective are nearly finished with their means of resistance. In about three months, they will have completed enough bows and arrows to attack the House Gods as they await their sacrifice. Their plan is to light the arrows on fire before flinging them across the canyon. Their goal is to burn the House Gods to the ground."

"It cannot possibly work," the neoclassical house said.

"I know," I agreed, "but that's not the point. Their act of resistance will inadvertently reignite the war. Their rebellion will be the first step toward eradicating humankind. After they attempt to set the House Gods ablaze, any plans for peace you and your comrades had been carefully concocting will dissolve."

"I see," the good House God said. "I thank you for coming, sincerely I do. The grave warnings you have passed on are undeniably helpful. We now have a timeline with which to work with, one that cannot be avoided. I will share what you said with the other House Gods as soon as you depart, and then we will collectively decide what to do."

"Will you though?" I asked. I didn't mean to say it. The thought just sort of fell into my mind. If we were speaking in words, the question would not have been asked.

"Will I what?" the House God asked.

I should have dropped it. But his question spurred the next thought. I couldn't help it. "Will you actually share any of this with the other House Gods? Will the good ones actually act? Or are you just saying this to me to appease me like you did to Devin?" I went on, "After all, my time will soon expire. What good would denying my requests do? If there is nothing you and your comrades can do to alter my future, would it not be better to allow me to hold onto hope?"

"This is an entirely different situation," The House God said. It didn't sound exactly mad, but it also didn't sound like its usual self.

"Is it?" I asked.

"Of course," it said. Maybe the House God was simply annoyed it had to spell out the differences of the two situations to me. "If we refused to help you, there would be other solutions you could find. They might not be ideal and they might not work, but you would have other options to explore. Devin, however, did not have any alternatives. His son was being sacrificed, not himself, and his son was under the control of The Coupling Caucus. If we refused him outright, there would be nothing else he could do. There would be nothing for him to hold onto. But aside from the logistics, you and Devin are entirely different beings. Your old friend believed in us because he thought we were the only reliable option, not because he believed we were the best. He had never attended your wife's meetings. He did not know what aspirations they contained. Once we let him down, whether we verbalized it or not, and his son had passed, he would reach for another form of resistance. You, on the other hand, already know the options. You have chosen us when no one else has, despite being aware of the alternate modes of resistance. So there would be no point in lying to you, Kurt, because you are on our side whether you like it or not. Because deep down, you truly believe a peaceful transition is the only possible path for a lasting solution."

"Okay," I said, all doubts of the House God's sincerity erased. "I will leave so you can share what you heard with the others. I will wait to see what you have decided, and will submit my fate to you and your comrades' walls."

"I'm happy to hear that," the House God said. "I will do all that I can to save you. But Kurt, it would be wise to avoid visiting us until after your scheduled day of sacrifice, should you be saved. As some of our comrades sacrifice themselves on your behalf, it'd be best for them and their closest friends, and consequently, for you, if they did not see you hanging around. They won't be the most stable houses, and there is no knowing what they might do if they saw the source of their instability."

I nodded. I understood what the House God's warning implied, and I accepted, however unhappily, the notion that I would not be seeing the white neoclassical House God, possibly my only true remaining friend, again until the day I was scheduled to die. Whether or not they would save my life would be an utter mystery to me until it happened. I kept nodding, and the House God led me from the red room and through its body before it expelled me out of its glass front door.

XXIII

I sat at our kitchen table as Katie prepared

for another CDC session. It was just under two weeks before my sacrificial ceremony was set to commence, and I had yet to readdress my refusal to resist. As far as Katie was concerned, it seemed she believed we were actually in agreement at the end of the CDC meeting nearly two months ago in which it was decided that the Repossesser would be unable to get me to appear at Harmony Crossing.

I obnoxiously cleared my throat, and when Katie glanced at me with rolled eyes, I said in a tone that sounded much braver than I felt, "You do understand that I will be attending my sacrifice, don't you?"

"What are you talking about, Kurt?" Katie asked. She sounded angry, but she looked worried.

"There is nothing you and your Collective can do to force me to miss my sacrifice," I said. "If I must, I will flee our tent before tonight's CDC session starts and will hide outside the city's perimeters until the time of my summons. I will do whatever it takes to be on Harmony Crossing at my appointed hour."

"But Kurt, why are you so intent on sacrificing yourself?" Katie asked, and she sounded sincere. "What are you hoping to achieve through your submission to the city and its murderous sacrifice system?"

"I have a plan," I said, "that I've been working on with the House Gods I believe to be good. Primarily, I plan to achieve peace. The good House Gods are in the process of building three mansions so big they will scrape the sky. They are sacrificing their own walls to construct them, and they are nearly complete. If they finish them before the time of my sacrifice, they will present them to the Founders, who are the House Gods that have been eating our people for centuries. When the Founders see these miraculous mansions, they will surrender, and the sacrifice system will cease to exist."

"But what if they don't finish these mansions in time? What happens then?"

"Then I die," I said. "But if that is the case, so be it. One day the mansions will be complete, and when they are, they will save humankind."

"But what if these House God saviors turn on their creators? What if they turn out even more evil than the Founders?"

I hadn't thought of that, and I hoped my facial expression didn't give away my surprise. I forced myself to cough in an attempt to cover it up, and instead of answering her question, I said, "Honestly, Katie, I just cannot fail to be at the bridge. I fear that if I refuse to show up, they will sacrifice our children in my place. And I could not live with myself knowing I was the sole reason more of our children died. So if my life will expire either way, why not save our children in the process?"

"There is no way of truly knowing whether or not The Coupling Caucus would send our children in our place. That's purely a hypothesis."

"But what if it's more?" I pleaded. "What if

this small-scale resistance sends more of our offspring to the bridge?"

"Goddammit, Kurt, don't you see that our children will inevitably be sent to Harmony Crossing if we refuse to resist? Sure, it might not be tomorrow, but the day they are selected for sacrifice will undoubtedly come. The only possible way we can guarantee their survival, not just for our children, but the children of generations to come, is to overthrow the current sacrifice system by any means necessary."

"I know that you believe that, and I even understand why you do. But just as strongly as you believe in your form of resistance, I believe in mine. I will not be a part of a rebellion that will inevitably resume the House God War. I will do everything in my power to overthrow the sacrifice system, but I will do it through a peaceful transition, albeit a forced one, via the presence of the astronomical mansions the House Gods are building."

"So you're essentially saying you will do absolutely nothing and simply hope the House Gods you believe are on your side won't betray you?"

"That's not how I'd put it, but if that's how you see it, then yes, that is my plan."

"Your plan is to achieve action through inaction," Katie said. "That's just excellent Kurt, I mean, what could go wrong?"

"If you love me at all anymore, then you will allow me to do what I must do. If you cannot promise that you and your Collective will not interfere with my plan, then I will leave our home this instant."

"I think you're a goddamn fool, Kurt. Truly, I do. And this ultimatum is absolute bullshit. But for reasons I cannot comprehend, I do. So you have my word that we will allow you to appear at your sacrifice, no matter how much it disappoints and infuriates us."

"Thank you," I said, and I tried to hug my wife, but she shoved me away.

Before we could say anything else, the first knock pressed into our canvas flaps, and my wife admitted the Andersons into the room. I poured myself a bowl of oyster soup topped with chili pepper flakes and lime juice and escaped to our bedroom where I ate alone. It was the first of two CDC sessions I would fail to attend. I refused to be a part of the Collective any longer. I wanted everyone in my wife's group to fully comprehend what side with which my priorities were aligned.

XXIV

My toes touch the grass on the House Gods' side of the canyon, and I'm surprised that I've stopped walking. As my heels lean back on Harmony Crossing, they uniformly repeat their call, "All hail the House Gods," and the Gothic house before me opens its front door.

I shift my gaze from the white neoclassical to the blue colonial, from the purple pueblo to the pink prairie, hoping to see the good House Gods preparing to reveal their superior plan. But what if this is not the right time? What if they haven't completed the mansions that will scrape the sky? What if they forsake me? My comrades seem to have faded into the background because all I see before me are front doors opening and closing repeatedly, and each time a door opens a House God's rug unrolls like a party horn before being sucked back inside as the door creaks closed. Maybe the white neoclassical and the others have disappeared into the trees to retrieve their astronomical mansions? I'm confident that any second now the good House Gods will act. Instead, the scents of peppermint and gingerbread, of campfires and cedar, magnify each time a door swings open as if the House Gods in front of me are coughing clouds. Their scents coalesce and I dream of being consumed by the Gothic House God that ate my son.

Somewhere in the back of my consciousness, somewhere the House Gods' alluring scents have yet to corrode, I think the good House Gods aren't going to save me. I think maybe my wife was right. I hear Katie's voice coming across the canyon, struggling in its swim through the rushing water, but by the time the sounds reach my ears her syllables have become meaningless susurrus. Still, her sound brings her sign to mind, and I tell myself that it is not too late.

I try to retrace my steps back to Harmony Crossing. I try to jump over the cliff into the water below. I close my eyes and envision myself walking backwards. I feel the ground change from the cushion of grass to the concreteness of wood. I open my eyes, and I see deep inside the Gothic House God's maroon door, see the rotting bodies of those who had entered before. I look down and see that my feet are carrying me across its porch. And as I cross the threshold into the House God's frame, greeted by my hanging son's decomposed corpse, my last thought suspends itself in my mind as if it were written on a sign.

Maybe, I think, some House Gods are good.

ABOUT THE AUTHOR

If Andrew J. Stone were a house, he'd be a tent. If he were a superhero, he'd be Marx. He is the author of the novella *The Mortuary Monster* (StrangeHouse Books, 2016) and numerous short stories and poems published in places like *New Dead Families*, *Hobart*, *Gutter Eloquence*, and *DOGZPLOT*, among others. He can be reached on Facebook (Andrew James Stone) and is currently living with his in-laws in Manhattan Beach, California. *All Hail the House Gods* is his second book.

Made in the USA
San Bernardino, CA
01 July 2019